"This writer takes no prisoners. With so much at stake she detours around pity and its lukewarm pals and cuts straight for the heart. What the hell is family, anyway? And what chance have we got to save one another? Pamela Shepherd writes with a clear eye and a strong love, and *Zach at Risk* is a necessary book."

—Summer Wood
Author, *Arroyo*

"Pamela Shepherd has written an honest, tender, and illuminating novel about people who've been left behind by America's mainstream. Zach, his lesbian mothers, and a gay man who stands in as Zach's father all struggle to heal and to reclaim their dignity. Despite seemingly impossible odds and personal failures, each ultimately triumphs, and together, they reinvent what it means to love, to be a family, and to create community."

—Alfred DePew
Author, *The Melancholy of Departure,*
A Wedding Song for Poorer People,
and *A Wild and Wooly Journal*
Writer's Sourcebook

"Pamela Shepherd has written a sometimes horrifying, but ultimately exhilarating novel about a nuclear family at the brink of disintegration. *Zach at Risk* follows the lives of five characters, all of them victims of sexual abuse: a mother, her lesbian partner (a carnival sword swallower), the son whom they nurture together, his best friend (a sometime street hustler), and the surrogate father, a neighbor who is dying of AIDS. Haunted by their personal horrors, each is tempted to repudiate the others, take flight, and self-destruct. But the most noble soul among them will take them through the portals of death where they will achieve their common redemption at 'the very core of kindness.' In vivid and unforgettable prose, Shepherd has shown us a path toward community that all of us must take if we are to find our way out of the sordid into the sacred."

—Pierre Delattre, MFA
Author, *Tales of a Dalai Lama,*
Walking On Air, Episodes,
Coming Home to Beauty,
and *Woman on the Cross*

Zach at Risk

HARRINGTON PARK PRESS
Alice Street Editions
Judith P. Stelboum
Editor in Chief

Zach at Risk

Pamela Shepherd

Alice Street Editions
Harrington Park Press®
An Imprint of The Haworth Press, Inc.
New York • London • Oxford

Published by

Alice Street Editions, Harrington Park Press®, an imprint of The Haworth Press, Inc., 10 Alice Street, Binghamton, NY 13904-1580.

PUBLISHER'S NOTE
This is a work of fiction. Names, characters, places, and incidents either are the products of the author's imagination or are used fictitiously, and any resemblance to actual persons, living or dead, business establishments, events, or locales is entirely coincidental.

Cover design by Marylouise E. Doyle.

Library of Congress Cataloging-in-Publication Data

Shepherd, Pamela.
    Zach at risk / Pamela Shepherd.
        p. cm.
    ISBN 1-56023-466-0 (soft cover : alk. paper)
   1. Teenage boys—Fiction. 2. Mothers and sons—Fiction. 3. Missing persons—Fiction. 4. Seattle (Wash.)—Fiction. 5. Lesbian mothers—Fiction. 6. HIV-positive men—Fiction. I. Title.
    PS3619.H457Z26 2003
    813'.6—dc21

2002154811

For
Nancy Stapp

The one thing in the world is spontaneous compassion. As for justice—that is a secondary matter.

Fyodor Dostoyevsky
Notebooks for *The Idiot*

Editor's Foreword

Alice Street Editions provides a voice for established as well as up-coming lesbian writers, reflecting the diversity of lesbian interests, ethnicities, ages, and class. This cutting-edge series of novels, memoirs, and nonfiction writing welcomes the opportunity to present controversial views, explore multicultural ideas, encourage debate, and inspire creativity from a variety of lesbian perspectives. Through enlightening, illuminating, and provocative writing, Alice Street Editions can make a significant contribution to the visibility and accessibility of lesbian writing and bring lesbian-focused writing to a wider audience. Recognizing our own desires and ideas in print is life sustaining, acknowledging the reality of who we are, as well as our place in the world, individually and collectively.

Judith P. Stelboum
Editor in Chief
Alice Street Editions

Acknowledgments

The writing of this novel has been a journey in community. My teachers, David Bosworth and Paula Bromberg, guided me in craft and understanding, and my dear friend and favorite poet, Sawnie Morris, read several versions of the manuscript and offered suggestions that were skillful and kind. Writing buddies Elizabeth Schilling, Ellen Levy, Kat Duff, Summer Wood, and Callie Williams provided much-needed support and assistance. My partner, Nancy Stapp, was generous in allowing the book to take up so much of our home and my time. Laurie Liss, my agent and friend, stayed with me through twelve years and three agencies. Poets & Writers, Inc. encouraged the beginning of this novel, and a generous award from the Astraea Foundation provided the time to see it through to the end. Thank you.

Dagg

Her first betrayal, Dagg would think much later, was that Zach had offered her the pattern that first day, but she had already been unable to see it. Just as she had failed to see the beautiful symmetry of Zach's first sand drawing—she had wanted to add a bottle cap, as if a manufactured RC cap had anything to do with what the boy was trying to say. Elliott Bay slapped black and cold against the gray-green sand and mud flats. Barnacles and mussels gripped the old tarred pilings as if clinging for their lives. Dagg walked beneath the pier looking for seashells or shiny stones to take home—her apartment was crowded with the treasures she'd found on this stretch of beach.

It was a cold and overcast, grayish day, which smelled beneath the old pier of salty tidal marshes, tar on wood pilings, and a not-too-clean industrial bay. Zach hunkered against a wood piling, a small, dark, six-year-old, clearly hiding from his mother. Beyond the fishing pier and pilings, where the low tide of the bay washed gently against the shore, a young woman paced frantically, calling the boy's name while her eyes scanned the cold black bay and the edge of the shore.

"Zach?" Dagg's first word to the boy had been his own name, but the boy shook his head, unwilling to claim it, then pointed to an oval-shaped design in the sand he'd been forming at his feet.

His finger had dug a moat three feet round, and inside the circle, twigs, mussel shells, and seaweed had been arranged in very specific patterns. The boy stared into the circle with her, then marched a shiny black mussel shell forward, jumped it onto a split green twig, and bashed the twig into the sand.

Later, Dagg would want to say that the boy was already telling the whole story, but she had been afraid already, unwilling to look carefully with him, unwilling to look either forward or back. Yet the story was laid out; Zach had framed it with his finger and left all the clues intact. But it would be years later when she would finally know that, and would want to go back there with him then, to walk back with the boy under the old abandoned pier, and hunker beside the black tar piling, and say, "Yes, Zach. Now I see it. Now what I see explains *everything.*"

Zach

"Zach!" The boy hunches over his knees by the craggy, black rocks of the sea wall, watching his mother call again as she paces amid the weathered gray pilings under the old pier. She is a tall, thin, young woman with a mane of sun-bleached hair blowing about a lightly freckled, sunburned face. Her eyes are pale green, like Zach's eyes. The tiger eyes and unruly hair are two things Zach clearly shares with his mother. From Zach's hiding place his mother's thin legs in their tight leggings look like toothpicks forking beneath an oversized brown bomber jacket. Zach watches his mother pace the narrow strip of beach between the jetty and the abandoned pier. Behind her Puget Sound laps softly onto mud flats and sand, its dank green water smelling of oyster beds and kelp, broken shells and diesel fuel. Patrice turns back toward the water; her thick hair whips about her face and she brushes it from her mouth in order to call his name one more time.

He is tall for a six-year-old, and broad shouldered; his wild dark curls cover his ears, framing a strong, intelligent face. His skin is still soft and hairless like a baby's; warm brown and lightly freckled, made startling when he smiles by the gigantic whiteness of three new permanent teeth. Zach is playing with his mother, but that is not all of it, because someone called him "nigger" today. This is a new word. A first word. In the way a word can take you out of yourself forever, and nothing will be quite right again.

Where the pier meets the rough wood bulkhead Zach hunkers down between the pilings, surrounded by the smell of old wood treated with creosote and tar. Nigger will smell like these things now: like the jetty and the bulkhead; like creosote, tar, and the salt of the bay; nigger will feel like sand inside his shoes would feel, rubbing him raw when he least expects it.

"Your dad was a black man. You are half black and half white—half of him and half of me." His mother tried to explain it this morning, but her words explain nothing, do not explain in himself the sudden lessening he feels. Nigger is not half of anything; it is a total word, divisive. Nigger defines what he is not as much as what he is now, and here, against the rough wood bulkhead, it is what he is *not* that is most disturbing. He is not like his mother, he knows for one thing. He is alone, Zach, nigger. He is not half but wholly this new thing, and his mother cannot help him learn how to be that.

Zach scrapes around the damp sand at the base of the piling until he has formed a smooth, flat circle of sand. From all around him he collects scraps of sticks and driftwood pieces, seaweed, mussel shells, and smooth, dark stones. With tools at hand, and his mother still calling, Zach begins to rebuild it here—his version of the story. He starts by creating the playground at school. He drives a twisted piece of twig hard into the wet sand—*there,* the boy stood *there,* next to the swing set Zach forms out of driftwood. Zach takes his position in front of the boy—he is a black shiny mussel shell upended; his open, alabaster insides face the hateful twig-stick boy.

Zach's mother calls again, but he continues to ignore her—he is building something here; this is important, what he's doing. Zach now marches the mussel shell forward, leaving half-moon prints as it leaps through the sand. When the mussel shell Zach reaches the twig-stick boy, the mussel shell knocks him and knocks him until the stick finally falls to the ground. Zach covers the stick with a seaweed blanket, then marches his shell-self backward and drapes him in rubbery green seaweed, like a cape.

The scene is over now. Zach rakes the cool sand clear with his fingers. He sets the mussel shell boy alone in the center.

"Zach! Quit goofing around! Zach!" His mother's voice is distant now. Zach looks down the beach where she frantically paces, and sees also, coming toward him, another figure on the beach. The woman hunches low over the wet rocks and leaps from them onto the bulkhead, before making her way piling to piling just as Zach did. She seems younger than Zach's mother, shorter and more wild-looking, with thick black hair tangled by the wind and blowing against her eyes and mouth. When she brushes it back out of her face, Zach sees that she is crying. She cries, he thinks, like grown-ups cry— silently and incidentally, as if no one, not even she, should pay attention. The woman watches Patrice over her shoulder as she hurries away from her, so intent on avoiding the woman on the beach that she doesn't notice Zach now crouching at her feet.

"Down here," Zach whispers. "She won't see you."

"Zach?" The woman looks down, startled by the thin, high voice of the child huddled against the wood piling, then notices his raked oval and stoops down next to him, as if to admire this thing he has made.

"It's nice," she says finally. The boy nods. The woman searches around beneath her and finally spies a bottle cap. "Here," she says, "do you want to put this in?"

Zach shakes his head; the cap is ugly—it has nothing to do with this thing he has made. Doesn't she see how the white sand dampens slowly to matte gray, how beautiful the seaweed is, lying across the bent twig child?

"Flotsam," the woman says, waving her hand across his circle. "They call that stuff flotsam and jetsam, for some reason."

Zach forms a blade with his left hand and uses it to reshape the frame around his story. When he finishes the border he rocks back on his heels. "There," he says, looking up at the stranger. He points to the flotsam playground, waving with his small, dark hand, as if the picture he has formed explains every single thing a boy could feel.

The woman stares down at his bits of twig and shell and seaweed now framed by the groove he has dug in the sand. She seems about to say something when Zach's mother calls again, then she looks out with him to where his mother now frantically runs along the shore. They watch silently for a moment together, and then the woman touches his shoulder. "Aren't you going to answer her?"

Zach wraps his arms around his knees and stares out toward the water. "You answer her," he says finally, picking up another shiny, black shell and setting it in the sand beside his.

"What?" The woman stares down at the two black shells standing upright in the sand.

"You be Zach," the boy says, finally. "You be Zach, now."

II

"Kamchatka against Irkutsk," Josiah pointed to Dagg's armies on Irkutsk. "She's sitting there with twenty-five armies."

"Not Irkutsk." Dagg waved her hand over the board, as if trying to distract him. "Zach knows better than that, for crissakes."

Zach cradled the four white dice in his hands and waited. Josiah and Dagg always argued at this point; it was their version of psychological warfare, which they thought worked with Zach because he was thirteen and they were grown-ups: each was sure they could argue long enough to finally convince Zach to attack the other.

"United Kingdom against Iceland," he said finally, shaking his dice at Josiah.

"Iceland," Josiah grumbled. He lay on his stomach on the living-room rug; a thin, petulant middle-aged child. "That's an easy move to make, isn't it? Twenty-one armies to two, four dice to one. You'll never hold Europe; no one holds it. Europe is a sucker trap in the middle of the world."

They'd started playing just after dinner, and now at eleven-thirty Zach held all of Europe and Asia, Dagg held the Americas, and Josiah was struggling to hold on to the rest. Zach loved the nights he played Risk with Dagg and Josiah. It was hard to put into words the peace he found in their games. There was the sameness of wood and plastic pieces moving on a cardboard map, the clattering of dice in the hand. Risk was sound and sight and texture; it called for little thought. He loved the bright red and yellow and blue of the world map, the warm smooth feel of the dice in his hands. While Zach played Risk the world retreated, shrank back for a moment to a board game, a thing that could be mastered and known.

Years later he would return in memory to that one evening—Josiah vital and alive beside him, Dagg's wonderful laughter still ringing through the house. Years later, he could still close his fists lightly, feeling in them the memory of the three warm dice—the sweep of his hand as he released them, the sound of them clattering onto the board.

"Your turn, Dagg." Josiah's voice sounded vaguely taunting. Her position on the board was bad and Josiah was moving in for a sweep. Dagg picked up the red dice and glanced at the clock for the third time that hour. "Her class is seven to nine; it's almost midnight." She rolled and lost two armies, then handed the still-warm dice to Zach.

Zach studied the board, shaking three dice softly in his hands. Josiah caught his eye for a moment, then quickly looked away toward the board. "Maybe she went to the library to study. The library doesn't close until eleven."

"Yeah, right. Eleven." Dagg pointed to Josiah's weakest spot on the board. "Zach, take him out in Western Australia. He's only got three armies left."

"Oh sure," Josiah grabbed the dice from Dagg's hand. "Take out your frustration on me, Dagg. Your girlfriend stays out late so you want the kid to wipe out the fag!"

Zach giggled and pointed to Australia. "OK against you, Josiah." He rolled and won all three dice, then rolled again and split two. Since Josiah had given him the game last Christmas, playing it had become an almost nightly ritual, which Zach often won because Josiah and Dagg constantly picked on each other. He had learned early that he could wait while they battered each other, then pick off their armies once they'd taken each other apart. Tonight it was especially easy because Josiah had nothing but bad luck and Dagg was clearly mad at Patrice and mostly seemed distracted.

Just past midnight, their game in full swing, they heard the downstairs door open and close softly and then heavy footsteps climb the stairs. Patrice staggered into the room looking exhausted, nodded to them slowly, stepped over Josiah's legs, and walked to the dining table to set down her schoolbooks. She looked at the game board and pieces strewn about the floor and smiled down at Zach, seated cross-legged almost at her feet. "I see you're teaching my son about domination, aggression, and violence."

Josiah nodded seriously. "Trying to make a man of him."

"Hi, Mom." Zach stretched his head back and looked up at her. "It's teaching me geography and I'm winning."

Dagg took up her dice and shook them hard. "Where were you?"

Patrice sighed and turned toward the kitchen. "Out, Dagg. I was out."

Josiah looked up from Australia, where his last army had just gone down in defeat. "What happened to your hair? It's orange."

Patrice removed the chopsticks that held her hair in a knot at the back of her head and let thick carroty curls fall loose to her shoulders. "What do you think?"

"It's orange." Dagg squinted up at her. "That class was over hours ago."

"I know. I know, Dagg. I had a couple of drinks with some friends—"

"But—"

"I like it," Zach interrupted, wanting to get between them with language, just as he'd pushed between them with his body when he was a child. "Talk about me," he used to insist when they fell into fighting, as if he knew that loving him was the only thing they could always agree on. Now he watched his mother take off her jacket and move about the living room, putting away books and setting water on the stove for hot tea, and he wanted his words to heal what he'd once tried to mend with his hands, pulling the women toward each other as if he could force them to touch and make up.

"You do like it, Zach? I was so depressed when I got off work. I stopped by Michael's and he helped me dye it."

"How did you choose that exact color?" Josiah motioned toward her hair with his dice. "I mean the Raggedy Ann motif and all."

"I was depressed, Josiah . . . now at least my hair is cheerful."

Zach laughed. "It is, and I like it. It makes you look like a floppy doll."

"A floppy doll?" Patrice looked worried for a moment, brushing back the loose strands from her face. "I don't think *that* is very attractive."

"Leave the game until tomorrow." Josiah yawned suddenly, stretching his long thin arms behind him. He often quit the game when he was losing to Dagg; tomorrow, if the board was still there—if Josiah hadn't managed to upset it; if half of Dagg's armies had not been mysteriously sucked up by the roving hose of the vacuum cleaner—they would discover Josiah's cards had managed to improve with sitting.

"I want to finish now," Dagg said. "You're almost wiped out; go ahead and surrender."

Patrice glanced at her watch. "Zach, it's almost midnight; you have school tomorrow."

"Just a minute, just a few more minutes. It's the last day of school anyway. Who cares if I'm awake or not?"

"It *is* late." Josiah yawned again. "Let's leave it until tomorrow."

"No way!" Dagg turned in another set of cards and began to break Josiah's last hold in South America. "Every time we leave these games your cards get better."

"Are you suggesting I cheat?" Josiah adjusted his silk gown like a campy Joan Crawford.

"You do cheat. It's a fact."

"I don't cheat . . . I strat-e-gize."

Zach stretched sleepily between them, barely listening as they argued, and no longer caring whether they finished the game that night or not. He felt peaceful and quiet while playing Risk with Dagg and Josiah, and lately, as things changed so quickly, it felt like the only place he could rest.

III

For years Zach had passed the store on his way home from school, and since he'd turned seven and was allowed to walk unescorted, he had often stopped at Shelby's to buy comic books, cheap toys, ice cream bars, or candy. Inside the store it was always dark, cool, and damp, smelling of humidors and fresh tobacco, the damp ink of fresh newspapers, and the crumbling must of old used paperbacks.

That afternoon, as always, Arthur Shelby stood patiently behind the back counter, his sightless blue eyes vacant and startled, as if the lights had just gone out on him and he'd been caught in perpetual surprise. As Zach opened the door the bells on top jangled, and from his place behind the counter the old man's head turned like a sunflower, his face curious and patient as he waited for a voice to follow.

"Afternoon, Mr. Shelby."

"Zach." The old man's face relaxed into a smile while his head dipped and bobbed as if the petals of his ears had caught a slight breeze.

Zach walked up and down the dim unlit aisles, his hands grazing thirty-five-cent water pistols and plastic clicker baskets that shot ping pong balls, while Mr Shelby's head turned and followed as if he could hear what Zach was seeing.

After carefully looking up and down each aisle, Zach ended his walk at the bookshelves under the front window, where he chose a *MAD* magazine. He returned to the back counter and began what for him was the most difficult part.

"I've got one magazine at $2.95, two Hershey Bars, and five red licorice. Here's five dollars, Mr. Shelby." Zach counted five singles into the old man's open hand. Zach always tried to bring Mr. Shelby singles because all bills felt the same, and he was afraid the blind man would think he was lying.

One morning last summer he'd been sent down to buy a newspaper by his mother, who'd given him a twenty-dollar bill and told him to bring change.

"Don't you have ones, Mom?"

"It's a store. They'll give you change, hon."

"But he can't *see* it's a twenty. He might think I'm lying."

Patrice had stopped dressing and turned toward Zach in exasperation. "It's his store, isn't it? If he thinks you're lying let him call the police."

So Zach had taken the twenty and laid it carefully on the blind man's glass counter. "My mom sent me to buy a paper. Here's a twenty-dollar bill."

Mr. Shelby had smiled and dipped as always, taking the bill without hesitation and giving him nineteen singles in change. Zach peeked into the cash register—it looked like everybody in the neighborhood paid everything in ones.

"How do you know it's really a twenty?" The boy gripped the edge of the counter and stared carefully forward. Sometimes he imagined that Mr. Shelby was not really blind. He was faking it to see who tried to cheat him. Then . . . Zach's imagination went wild here, but usually involved being chased by Mr. Shelby wielding long, sharp knives.

Mr. Shelby smiled. "I can feel the difference."

"In the paper?"

"In the boy."

Zach released his grip from the counter and exhaled slowly. It was true, then; he could smell liars. Zach stepped back one step and stretched for his money. Shoving the thick wad of ones into his jeans pocket, he said, "Yeah, well, Mr. Shelby, I gotta go now." Mr. Shelby's moon face turned and nodded, his smile diligent and precise as a child's.

Today Zach paid with his stack of singles and picked up his paper bag, which Mr. Shelby had expertly folded and handed to him across the counter. Zach felt the extra weight of it and wondered what the old man had added today. Ever since he was a little kid the old man had added something: a butterscotch candy or jawbreaker, sometimes a single piece of gum.

"Oh, Zach," Mr. Shelby said.

"Yes."

"I heard the children talking this morning. Are you finished with school now, for the summer?"

"Today was the last day, yeah." Zach turned back toward the old man politely, trying not to notice how the pale, immobile face gave him the creeps.

"I could use some help here sometimes. In the afternoons some days. I'd like a boy I know I can trust. Do you think you'd be interested?"

"I have to ask my mom, I guess." Zach looked around the store again, trying to imagine spending hours alone with the old man inside it. The thought made him feel squeamish, but he couldn't say why. "I'll ask her tonight. I gotta go now."

Mr. Shelby listened in his odd slow way, as if his hearing had more depth than most people's, as if it took an extra moment for Zach's words to go all the way in. And maybe, Zach thought, that's why peo-

ple talk loud and funny to blind people, always enunciate too clearly
to be quite polite. Now, after an interminable pause, Mr. Shelby nodded. "Let me know soon, though. I want someone who can start next
week."

Patrice had been pleased when Zach took the job helping Arthur
Shelby. "It's good for him," she told Josiah and Dagg. "He needs a father figure, a man in his life."

"What am I? The resident petunia?"

"You know what I mean, Josiah. I mean someone more authorita-
tive, more stately."

"More straight, you mean." Josiah sprawled across the couch eating
carrot sticks while Dagg and Patrice made dinner. "John Wayne, slightly
disabled."

"That's not what I meant."

"You don't have to tell me, I've seen *Red River.*"

Josiah owned Vintage Video on Fremont Avenue, and it seemed to
Zach that Josiah's whole world was filtered through those old-time
movies. If Zach hadn't watched so many of them from Josiah's couch
in the apartment behind them, most of Josiah's conversations would
have made no sense at all. Now he looked at Josiah, wondering if the
thing Patrice said had hurt his feelings. "You want something to
drink, Josiah?" Zach took a can of root beer from the fridge and held it
in the air between them.

Josiah laughed and waved it away. "What do you think, Zachy? Is
the blind old man stately or not?"

Zach put the can of root beer back into the fridge, trying to think
how to answer him. He knew he didn't have to answer, that really
Josiah was just joking, but he closed the refrigerator door slowly, trying to form the thought in his head. "I think he's—" he started to say,
but Dagg interrupted.

"The guy gives me the creeps," she said.

"That's because he's blind." Patrice set the chicken casserole in the
middle of the table. "That's what makes you uncomfortable. People
get uncomfortable around the disabled."

"I don't think that's it, Patrice." Dagg looked at Zach curiously, but he felt her gaze and looked away, carefully keeping his eyes averted. *I think he's sad,* Zach wanted to say. *I think he's really sad and lonely.*

Zach went to his new job at two every afternoon and stayed until they locked up and counted out the money. Somebody from the bank would come by at five and take the bank bag to the night deposit, and Zach would dust and sweep and then say good night. He would take a candy bar from the counter and walk home eating it, arriving a few minutes before Patrice or Dagg served dinner. He kept thinking he would get more used to the old man, but he didn't. He didn't like his smell, for one thing, or the way Mr. Shelby stood too close to him behind the counter. Still, he felt more confused than bad about it, and sometimes when he watched the way strangers talked to Mr. Shelby he felt sorry again for him. Some people talked loud and slow like the old man was deaf or an idiot; some used small simple words like he was a very old child; and some, not expecting a blind man, would flush, put down their packages, and leave without buying.

Zach's job was to watch casually as customers paid, and to tell Mr. Shelby if the bills weren't what they said. He felt like he took care of Mr. Shelby—that somehow the old man needed all the help he could get—but Zach felt a little guilty also; he had felt in himself his own temptation and believed that others must also be tempted.

That Friday while Zach removed books from the shelves and dusted, Mr. Shelby spoke to him from the back of the room, his voice less eerie now, its echo-chamber quality more familiar. "Put the numbers of the Hardy Boys in the right order, Zach. I don't know why people have to mess them up."

"I got that already." Zach glanced back toward the old man, shadowed now behind the counter. "Mr. Shelby?"

"Yes."

"Have you always been blind? I mean . . . could you ever see things?"

"I could see shadows and gray when I was younger. I used to see some light and movement. But 'pitch black the night descends/ falling among the rustling branches/ young boys move home/ toward outstretched arms of anxious mothers.' Things go. I wanted to be a poet once, that's why I bought this store. I intended to sell literature and write great poetry. Life never goes like we plan, Zach. People didn't want literature; they wanted cigarettes and chocolate, detective books and breath mints."

"Do you still write poems, Mr. Shelby?" Zach secretly hoped that he didn't. When people read poems you were supposed to set your face in a certain way and listen like it meant something. When Patrice took English literature last semester she walked around for days repeating, "Tyger! Tyger! burning bright/ In the forests of the night," in a loud fakey sounding voice, and got real mad at Dagg and Josiah when they didn't find the whole thing uplifting.

"Tiger tiger burning bright. . . . Who set the candle in your ass alight . . ." Josiah's version was better—he kept repeating it in whispers while Zach and Dagg almost died trying to hide their laughter.

"Barbarians!" Patrice had stomped off to English class, where, Dagg and Josiah agreed, she probably had the hots for her teacher, a greasy-haired troll with a fake English accent, and Zach had decided, but not told anyone, that when it came to literature he was on the side of the barbarians.

Mr. Shelby smiled his slow, shy moon-smile. "Poetry belongs to young men. It's enough now I have my music."

Zach felt guilty relief, as if he'd managed to squirm out of something; he'd been so afraid he'd have to hear it. The music Mr. Shelby liked was also boring and stuffy, but Zach didn't feel quite so squirmy about it. The faded red radio in the kitchen played softly all through the day, tuned forever to the classical station. Soft wordless music played continuously, interrupted on the hour and half hour by a quiet, sleepy-sounding man who announced the names of the pieces and gave updates on the time and weather. Whenever the store was empty, or when Zach was there to watch the cash register, Mr. Shelby sat on a stool in the doorway to the kitchen, listening, his head turning and nodding like a slowly aging flower.

Now the radio played some choral piece sung by an English church choir, and Mr. Shelby leaned against the back wall, his head thrown back, humming along in a vaguely off-key sort of way. When the chorus finished, he smiled and sat forward. "I always think of that as

Christmas music; how odd to hear it in July. It's beautiful, don't you think, Zach?"

Zach nodded, then, remembering the old man couldn't see him, said, "Yeah, I guess so." It seemed sad to him mostly, the saddest music. For some reason the music made him feel lonely.

"What's Christmas like at your house, Zach?"

The boy thought for a moment, trying to remember if any two holidays had ever been alike. "I don't know. Last year Josiah, my neighbor, cooked a turkey. We ate a lot and then opened presents. I got a Risk game from Josiah." Zach finished sweeping, then reached behind the counter to find the dustpan. "Where's your family, Mr. Shelby?"

"I had a sister. I used to spend holidays with her and her family, but . . . we had a falling out a few years ago. Don't ever get old, Zach, that's my advice. Whatever you do, don't ever get old."

Zach dumped the dustpan of dirt into the trash can. "I'm going to take the trash out. You have any more in the back to take?"

The old man seemed lost in some long-ago memory. "They say your family will love you forever, but it isn't true. There's nothing magic about blood relations. . . . There are things that can make just anybody hate you."

Zach nodded, mentally adding Mr. Shelby to his next year's Christmas list. Maybe Josiah would help him find a classical tape or an opera or something. "I used to want a little brother," he said haltingly, "but my mom said that Dagg couldn't . . ." He stopped, suddenly reminded that his family didn't translate. "Anyway, I never got one; only now I have my friend Josiah."

He thought of Josiah standing in his tiny kitchen last Christmas, basting a turkey the size of a plump, short-legged dog. Joan Armatrading played loudly on the stereo, and Josiah sang along in his off-key voice, dancing awkwardly from stove to sink and back again, while instructing Zach how to make potato casserole and how to make a relish tray with carrot slivers, radishes, celery, and small cocktail onions.

They had eaten themselves sick that day, and then walked down to Gasworks Park and thrown rocks out from the jetty into the cold gray froth of Lake Union. That was the night Josiah taught them how to play Risk; Zach loved it from the beginning, Dagg couldn't get enough, and Patrice quit midway through the first game and would never play again.

"It's stupid," she said. "All that time and energy wasted, and then at the end you've just played a game. If you ever focused that much passion into your own life, you could get anywhere, Zach. You could change your life forever."

But Zach hadn't wanted to change his life; he liked it, mostly. And he loved best the nights he played Risk with Dagg and Josiah—so much concentration and attention and passion, and yet nobody really fought to be mean. They bickered, sure—they argued and picked because they liked to. That was really the very best part of the game.

"Zach. Would you take this, too?" Mr. Shelby was trying to hand him a knotted plastic trash bag, and Zach took it from his outstretched hand, set the broom back behind the counter, and carried the trash and the small bag from beside Mr. Shelby's bed out to the dumpster in the alley in back.

Coming in through Mr. Shelby's kitchen a few minutes later, he heard someone at the counter talking to the old man. "Two packs of Camels, please. I'll take three Snickers bars and this lighter. Here's a twenty. You wouldn't happen to sell Dunhills, would you?"

Zach pushed the curtain aside and looked across the counter at a thin dark-skinned boy who smiled pleasantly at him while holding a crisp new one-dollar bill toward the old man. The boy seemed completely sure of himself and smiled sweetly at Zach as if they were old friends, sharing a wonderful joke on the old man.

Zach moved forward, touching Mr. Shelby's arm with his hand. "It's a one, Mr. Shelby."

"You fuckhead!" The boy dropped everything on the counter. "Don't leave this store if you want to live!" He turned and ran out the front door, while Mr. Shelby turned his head slowly, trying to follow the sounds, as if he couldn't quite keep up with the action.

When Zach left to go home a few hours later the boy was waiting for him, leaning against the narrow brick between storefronts, one foot resting flat on the wall behind him. He was older than Zach, and about the same height, but delicate and graceful where Zach was broad and chunky. His face was russet brown and heart shaped. His eyes were wide apart and almond, framed with thick black lashes that turned up at the edges as if the boy had been born wearing mascara and lived on the verge of perpetual surprise.

Zach curled his fists unconsciously and moved toward the older boy. He wasn't eager, but he was willing to fight him. As he approached, the other boy smiled lazily, stretching his arms above him along the warm brick wall. "So who is he, your grandpa or something?"

"No."

"You're kind of like the black Batman. You save blind guys in distress." This last was not a question, but as if the boy was flirting with him.

"Don't you think it's kind of terrible, ripping off a blind guy?"

"I could hardly have done it if the old man could see." The boy laughed. "Can't you imagine?

—Here's a twenty.

—No it's not, it's a one.

—No, it's a twenty!

—What do you think I am, blind?"

Zach laughed in spite of himself, relieved he didn't have to fight now. It wasn't fear . . . the guy was little and, if not feminine exactly, sort of delicate and wild.

"I'd a made sixteen bucks off that guy plus the stuff I was buying, until you came in and blew it for me."

"I can't believe you said it was a twenty."

"You'd a come in anyway, right? There I'd be chumping a blind man for change. You get caught all the same for a five or a fifty."

"Then why didn't you say it was a fifty?"

"The man's blind, he isn't stupid. Raul Martinez. I know I'm wild but you mustn't be frightened." Zach laughed and shook his offered hand. "You're a child," Raul said. "I see that. I'm fifteen and in the theater."

"Theater?"

"Pro-jec-tion-ist, actually." He said the word syllabically, as if he personally was responsible for the manifestation of images on the screen. "You know the old Ridgemont?"

"The porn house?"

Raul nodded as if the conversation was starting to bore him. "I run that."

"The theater?"

"The projector. And we only show porn on weekdays; on weekends we show foreign and art films. Have you ever seen *Camille*? I love that movie! I know the guy who owns the theater. He lets me sleep there if I run the projectors. I've seen more dirty movies than a child like you could ever imagine."

"I'm not a child."

"How old? Thirteen? You're a very big strong little boy. Come on, I left a bottle of Mad Dog in the bushes. If we cut across to the school playground, no one can see us from the street." He took Zach's arm and led him across the street to the middle-school playground, a blank square of asphalt, basketball hoops, four square courts, and picnic tables. "I got this from a trick last night. I . . . hmmmm . . . trick sometimes for extra money."

"With guys? You do it with guys?"

"Women won't pay, dear. Women are prudish about relationships, especially the relationship between sex and money. They don't mind that they're related; they just think a guy should pay them for it. Why is that anyway? The guy does all the work; chicks just have to lay there and wheeze. But when men want sex they pay for it. I thought they'd be fags when I started but it's almost always married guys.

"I had one guy last week. A preacher from some holy-roller church in White Center, he wanted me to pray with him after he blew me. I said, You're already on your knees, man. You just take care of it.

"I did have a woman pay me once. Have some more of this wine, Zachy. She pulled up in front of Penny's in a silver Mercedes; asked me if I wanted to go have a party." Raul stopped, as if considering how the story should go next. "So I said fifty, you know.

" 'What do I get?' she asks, kind of flirty. Women shouldn't ever go flirty when they're over thirty; it makes them look really disgusting.

"I said, 'You get everything. Everything you want.'" Raul bit his lower lip and grinned at Zach. "You like this story so far?"

"Yeah."

"So I went home with her, to Bellevue. She had this incredible house on the lake. And this yard like Volunteer Park or something, huge trees, rolling lawn, magnolias, and azaleas. I'm kind of excited now, you know. At first I was kind of nervous, but jeez, I think she wants me, and she wants it kind of all romantic.

"'Can I get you something to drink?' she asks. Like the movies, right?

"'Champagne,' I say. She looks at me like she thinks that's funny but I'm thinking already, I'm thinking I'm gonna do her with champagne on her. I'm gonna pour champagne all on her and then really fuck her lights out.

"So we take this champagne and walk down across the grounds to the edge of the water, and it's real soft and sweet, lapping at the dock. And I lay down on a blanket she brings out, and I'm so fucking hot by now I really want to fuck her.

"'Oh baby,' she's moaning, 'fuck me hard.' She wants me so bad it's torture. She's rolling around all under me trying to get fucked even better.

"I banged her fucking sore, man. I fucked her till her head rolled. Real romantic. Then she paid me fifty bucks and told me to get lost.

"You like that story? Look, your dick's hard. Didn't think you were old enough to get a hard-on."

"I want to meet someone like her," Zach said quietly.

"You will, man. Women love black guys; they're gonna beg you for it."

IV

Zach got home just before midnight, enduring a terrible queasiness in his stomach from his share of the wine. In the living room Josiah stretched out on the couch like a man in rigor mortis, his blue-white legs looking like a newly plucked chicken. He and Dagg were watching *Saturday Night Live* and arguing about whether it had ever been funny. Both agreed it was not funny now, but Josiah insisted it had been once. "Land Shark was funny. The Coneheads were funny. But this . . ."

"Josiah, this show was never funny. Nothing about this was ever funny."

"I used to think . . ."

"You used to be high. Stoplights were funny. I remember being on mescaline one time when hubcaps were the funniest thing in the world." Dagg sat on the rug, resting her back against the couch, letting Josiah's legs stick past her like the arms to a ridiculous chair. A six-pack of Rainier Beer cans lay strewn across the coffee table, along with a crumpled bag that had once held nacho chips. Zach balanced carefully in the doorway, trying not to sway or slur. He thought they seemed as drunk as he felt, but that didn't mean they wouldn't notice. "Hi, you guys."

He thought he sounded normal enough, but Josiah straightened on the couch and stared up at him for a long time. "Speaking of motherhood, Zach's been drinking. What have you been drinking, son?"

"You're not my father." Zach pushed Josiah's legs aside and squeezed down next to him on the couch.

"Not your father," Josiah said softly. "Fuck not . . . look at my legs! Where's Patrice when we need her? We need a role model here."

Zach started to giggle. "You're drunk, Josiah. I'm sorry about your legs."

"You're sorry! I'm sorry! Oop . . . Mama's home. Now we're in trouble!"

Patrice had come up the stairs without them hearing and now stood in the doorway holding two sacks of groceries. "What's going on?"

"Just what we needed. A mother!" Josiah started to giggle again.

"Who got you drunk, Zach? Which of you reptiles got my son drunk?"

"We are . . ." Dagg straightened, "an innocent terrarium. He managed it all by himself and so did we."

"Zach! Go to bed. We'll discuss this in the morning."

"He's thirteen," Josiah said. "He probably smokes, too. Probably keeps a crush-proof box of Marlboros in the bushes."

Zach smacked Josiah's leg. "I do not!"

"Josiah, just stay out of this."

"Patrice, you're very funny when you're playing June Cleaver." Josiah motioned to her carrot-orange hair, wild on her head, her chartreuse men's sport coat with the sleeves rolled up, black capri pants, and sports bra.

"You don't look like Mrs. Cleaver," Dagg said solemnly. "You look sort of nasty."

"Where have you been in *that* outfit?" Josiah ignored Dagg's and Zach's giggles and cocked one hand on his hip in simulated anger.

"I am trying to finish school this semester. I am trying to get somewhere in my life!"

"You studied algebra in *that* outfit?" Josiah's June Cleaver imitation was better than Patrice's.

Zach, meanwhile, ignored his mother and lay down on the couch with his head on Josiah's thigh. Dagg straightened the afghan over both of them, tucking it tightly under Zach's chin. "There used to be a thing called tragedy," she said softly. "Now there is only television."

Zach fell asleep to the feel of Dagg's cool hand against his forehead. He knew vaguely that he was in trouble, but his mother's sharp voice barely penetrated into his sleep. The next day Patrice woke Zach early, and he staggered from his bed feeling nauseous and slow with what was not exactly a hangover, but a feeling as if he'd eaten too much candy.

"Where did you get the wine?" Patrice started in immediately while setting out cereal and milk and bananas for breakfast.

"Some guy."

"Who?"

"I don't know."

"What did you drink?" Dagg had decided on a sideways approach.

"Mad Dog."

"Oh God, your liver!"

"It tasted like. . . ." Zach paused, sucking on the insides of his cheeks as if the taste might remain and help him remember. "Like grape juice that's been puked already." He smiled slightly, delighted to find a description perfect and exact.

"You liked that?"

"I didn't *like* it." Zach looked at his mother as if he were just beginning to suspect the depths of her stupidity. "We chugged it. I just held my breath and drank it fast. It made me laugh. I liked laughing. We laughed and Raul—"

"Who's Raul?"

"Nobody. Some guy I met." Zach was quiet, losing interest in this interrogation. "I liked him. I feel pretty awful now, though." Zach was thinking about Raul, his mysterious new friend, who knew how to get wine and got paid money to *do* rich ladies. He avoided the word *fuck* here; fuck had always been a casual word, a word he'd grown up with. What Raul did to rich ladies belonged to that word suddenly, made it frightening and meaningful and, for the first time, much too real.

"Of course you feel bad. It's called a hangover." Patrice took Zach's chin between her hands. "I don't want you drinking, Zach. It's not right for you to do."

Zach nodded slowly. "I think I'm getting a cold or something. Maybe I'll just go back to bed."

Patrice kissed him on the cheek and pushed him toward his bedroom. "I have to leave for work. I'll see if Josiah will check in on you later."

Josiah agreed, as he always did, to keep an eye on Zach that morning, though his idea of "keeping an eye on" was much more casual than Patrice and Dagg would ever imagine. He poked his head into Zach's room sometime after eleven and asked the boy if he was still sleeping. Zach lay curled in a ball on his side, facing the doorway; he opened his eyes slowly and moaned.

"Very dramatic." Josiah leaned against the doorway, his overlong frame having to slump sideways a little so as not to knock his head. "At noon they're showing *Johnny Guitar* on the Movie Channel. If you're still alive you can watch it from my couch."

Zach moaned again but perked up. His throat did seem to be getting slightly better. "I don' know." he said stuffily.

"You don' know what?"

"If I can," the boy explained, already starting to grin.

"Well, if you can't you can't, but I thought I might call out for pizza."

By noon Zach had wrapped himself in his favorite blanket and sprawled across Josiah's couch, looking theatrically hung over. Josiah had called out for pizza, and he poured the boy a root beer and opened the pizza box between them.

"It's not a veggie, is it?" Zach's stuffed-up nose made him sound like he was talking through a tunnel.

"Veggie? Do I look like a pizza barbarian?" Josiah lifted out a slice of pepperoni and laid it on a paper towel in front of the boy. "Sit up to eat. I can't stand drooling. Oh there she is, Bitch of the West, Mercedes McCambridge! This is a great movie, a classic. . . . Look at Joan Crawford, that butch thing!"

Although Patrice was lately always asking Josiah to "talk to that boy," their conversations were almost always like this one. Josiah would recount the plots of his favorite old movies while Zach grinned and listened and drank too much pop. Now Zach felt restful and happy with Josiah, lying under his blanket, filled with pizza, watching *Johnny Guitar*. He felt happy when he was with Josiah because Josiah didn't care whether Zach talked or not, and he was now entertaining himself by repeating all the worst lines of the movie. "That's big talk for a little gun," Josiah roared. "Don't you love this movie, Zach? You want more pop? I have cola, cream, or lemon-lime."

"Nothing. I don't feel good."

"Well, go back to bed then." Josiah leaned against the base of the couch, framing the television between his bony knees. His mothering ability, like their conversations, was almost nonexistent.

"My mother said you should watch me." Zach felt bad enough to sound childish.

"Your mother acts like you're a baby. No kid should ever have two mothers, and especially not a boy. It's not that they're lesbians, I mean. It's women." He spoke as if women lived beyond an endless, mysterious sea. "They always want to talk about everything, they always want you to 'share your feelings.' Everyone has feelings, Zach, but they're sort of like colds—it's not always polite to spread them around."

Zach laughed, relieved a little to hear someone express what he'd already suspected. Josiah sat up, feeling momentarily wise and parental; it pushed him further than he probably should have gone alone. "When you're older, Zach, and with a girl, don't let her talk about sex. There's a certain amount of energy in us; it either goes to talk or fucking."

He lay back against the couch again, as if his foray into heterosexuality had exhausted him, and Zach retreated, confused and betrayed, as if he'd been given more information than any thirteen-year-old could use. Zach stared past Josiah as if across another mysterious sexual sea, not because Josiah was gay but because he was thirty.

V

Zach worked through June and July and into August. He would organize things in back for Mr. Shelby, stock shelves, dust bookcases, sweep the faded hardwood floors, and take the trash out back to the dumpster. When he was through he'd take a free candy bar from the rack, and the back issues of magazines Mr. Shelby set aside for him, then walk the four blocks home to Dunlop Street eating his candy bar and clutching the thin brown paper sack in which Mr. Shelby always put his magazines.

Sometimes Josiah would be home when Zach got there and they'd play horse in the back alley under a basketball hoop Dagg had put up when he was seven, the year the Sonics won the NBA championship. Sometimes Zach would come home to find the place empty, and he would lock himself in his bedroom and look at his magazines until somebody else got there. Evenings he often walked up Fremont to meet friends at Tower Records or the doughnut shop, or he'd take his basketball to the middle school and try to find a pickup game. Sometimes he'd run into Raul and they'd go hang out in the University District or climb the fence into Woodland Park Zoo.

This afternoon Raul was waiting for Zach outside Shelby's when he got off work, leaning against the same brick wall where Zach had first met him. He fell into step beside Zach, taking the offered Snickers bar and eating half of it in one bite. "What's in the bag, Zachy?"

"Magazines." Zach shifted the package under his left arm and took back what was left of his candy.

"Like porn mags? Are they dirty? What kind of magazines?"

"Fuck you." Zach walked faster, turning the corner at 41st and heading toward Dunlop.

"*Penthouse? Hustler?*" Raul laughed. "You got a *Playgirl* in there for your fag neighbor?" He grabbed Zach's arm and tried to pull the package away. Zach shrugged him off and pushed him, sending the older boy stumbling off of the curb. "Okay, okay! I was just asking." Raul got back in step beside him.

"It's nothing, okay? Just back issues."

"Well, then, come on. Let me see it."

Zach shrugged, opening the top of the sack and pulling an old *Car and Driver* magazine up from the top.

"A car magazine? A motorhead publication?" Raul looked disgusted.

"You're so stupid." Zach rolled down the top on his sack again and started to jog toward the corner. When Raul kept up with him, Zach began to run faster until they sprinted the last half block to the house and raced up the stairs together, each shoving at the other, trying to be first to the apartment.

Inside, Zach pushed Raul down onto the couch before putting his jacket and package in the bedroom and shutting the door. Raul picked up the remote control and flicked through the stations a few times before finally getting bored with it and opening the refrigerator. "Want something to drink?"

"Root beer."

"Yeah sure. What is this—Rainbow Pop?"

Zach pushed past him into the kitchen and began searching the cupboards for something to eat. "Josiah gets it wholesale through his business."

"He can't spend two cents more for a fucking real Coke?"

Zach laughed, popping open the can Raul handed him and taking the root beer, a bag of potato chips, and half a bag of Oreos into the living room, where he shoved Raul aside and sprawled next to his friend on the couch.

"What time does your mom get home?"

Zach shrugged. "It doesn't matter. You can stay, you know, and meet them."

Raul glanced away, sucking on his root beer. "I don't know if that's such a good idea, Zachy."

Zach stared at Raul's head, feeling somehow older for a moment, and also suddenly fierce and protective. Every time he met Raul that feeling seemed to grow inside him—that the older boy was not as tough as he wanted to seem. Sometimes he felt like Raul was his younger brother, and it was Zach's job to somehow protect him. "They'll like you," he said finally. "They like weird people."

Dagg and Patrice came home from work at six, and Josiah showed up a few minutes later. Josiah stared at Raul a long time, like he was trying to remember something, then finally asked, "Have we met, Raul? You look awfully familiar to me."

The boy tugged at the legs of his shorts, crossing his legs in a way that was deliberately campy. "I don't know where we could have met, do you?" He smiled mockingly. Josiah collapsed into the blue armchair, his legs stretched out before him, staring at Raul ferociously, like Zach was a girl on a first date and Josiah her distrustful, middle-aged dad.

In the kitchen Patrice and Dagg stared at Zach strangely. "This is the kid you admire most in all the world?" Patrice turned away and began to put away groceries while Dagg started grilling hamburgers and onions for dinner.

"Maybe he's just gay." Dagg stared past Patrice toward the boy on the sofa. "Maybe they're—"

"Dagg! The kid looks like a hooker, for crissakes."

Dagg snorted, trying to hide her laughter. "I'm sure he's just a nice young man in mascara."

"Stop it!" Zach wanted to hit them. "You don't know anything about him."

"Some things you just know, Zach."

"You do not! Nobody does."

"I'm sorry, Zach. You're right. We don't know him." Patrice handed him a handful of silverware. "Now set the table, please, and ask Raul what he wants to drink."

Zach set the silverware and napkins down on the table and asked Raul what he wanted to drink. Raul smiled slowly at Josiah. "Campari on ice would be nice." He crossed his legs, hooking one foot behind his calf so that his bare legs in his short shorts looked like a shapely twisted pretzel.

Josiah stood up slowly and limped toward the kitchen, pausing in the doorway to look back at the boy. "You can have milk, water, or root beer."

"Root beer would be nice . . . if it's that delicious Rainbow brand." Raul winked at Zach who tried to stifle a laugh. He'd never seen Josiah act like such a jerk.

Patrice served hamburgers on onion buns, potato salad, and carrot sticks, and they ate awkwardly at the table, avoiding the boys' eyes and glancing, bewildered, at each other whenever they thought the boys were not looking.

"What school do you go to?" Dagg cut her hamburger into quarters and lifted a quarter section to her mouth.

"I'm out."

"Graduated?"

Raul smiled slowly, cutting his eyes to look at her. "In a manner of speaking."

"What manner of speaking?" Josiah leaned forward across from him, resting his elbows on the table and linking his hands together, forming a triangle over his plate.

"I quit. I graduated myself."

Patrice glanced at Dagg who stared curiously at Zach. "How old did you say you were?"

Raul smiled at her tauntingly. "I didn't."

Patrice passed him the bowl of potato salad. "Another hamburger, Raul?"

Josiah leaned on his elbows, edging slightly forward. "What do your parents do?"

Raul bit into another hamburger and answered with his cheeks stuffed full. "I don't really know. I haven't seen either of them in some time."

Josiah cleared his throat and sat back. Raul smiled at him while taking another mound of potato salad onto his plate. "I feel like we're in *Guess Who's Coming to Dinner*. You make a lovely Spencer Tracy."

Josiah set his fork down suddenly like he was going to explode, but Patrice touched his arm and interrupted. "Zach's only thirteen. He looks old for his age." She tried to sound conversational but her voice held an edge that turned the words into some kind of warning.

"And a very handsome boy he is too." Raul kicked Zach's leg under the table, and Zach stared down at his plate, afraid if he caught anyone's eye he'd either scream or start laughing.

Raul, seemingly more entertained than upset by their discomfort, finished his dinner slowly, then moved back into the living room, collapsing into the blue armchair. Dagg sat near him on the couch, staring curiously at his black-lined eyes, until, leaning forward, she asked suddenly, "Is that tattooed on there?"

The boy giggled, his voice soft and girlish. "Do you like it?"

Dagg glanced at Patrice, who looked over at Josiah, who stared at Raul with his arms crossed, looking as if, for the first time in his life, he could not think of a thing to say.

Patrice finally stood up. "There's ice cream for dessert," she said, taking refuge in the kitchen.

Dagg, Josiah, Zach, and Raul sat quietly, looking everywhere but at each other. "Zach, go help your mom," Josiah said finally.

"But—"

"Go . . . Dagg . . . you go with him." Josiah stood up and paced back and forth between the door and the window. When the others were gone and he was alone in the room with Raul, he walked over to the boy's chair, leaned over him, and whispered softly, "I'm sure you're a decent kid, Raul, but if you get Zach in any trouble I'll break both your arms."

Raul recoiled as if someone had hit him, then recovered himself, cut his eyes sideways at the much taller man, and smiled a lazy, taunting smile. "Oh, grandmother, what big teeth you have!" He stood up, brushed at the legs of his short shorts as if to straighten them, and strolled slowly to the door. "I have to be going now, Zachy!" he called toward the kitchen, and then, flashing a bitchy smile toward Josiah, let himself out the door.

Zach heard their exchange and then the door slamming. He ran into the living room, shoved Josiah out of his way, and ran to the window. "Wait!" he called down to Raul. "Wait, I'm coming!"

Josiah rested a hand on Zach's shoulder. "Let him go, Zach—"

Zach pushed his hand away and wheeled around to face him. "What did you say to him? You treated him like garbage! How could you treat my friend like that?"

"Zach, the kid is—"

"Fuck you, Josiah!" Zach pushed past him, then grabbed his jacket and followed his friend out the door.

They walked down Fremont to the bike path and then along the path skirting north of Lake Union, past Gasworks Park, toward the University Bridge. Along the path wild blackberries were ripening, and the boys waded through waist-high bushes to find the small blue-black berries which left purplish stains in the palms of their hands. Occasionally a street lamp would cut the darkness, illuminating a large soft oval of the berry bushes with a phosphorus pink. They would stop then and search out new handfuls, laughing and talking with their mouths full and stained red.

Raul took a pack of Marlboros from his jean jacket, placed a cigarette in his mouth, and handed the pack to Zach, who tapped a filter against the back of his wrist, backhanded the cigarette to his mouth, and lit it, exhaling the first wisp of smoke through his nose. "I hate how they acted." Zach slowed his pace slightly so Raul could keep up.

"Forget it." Raul bent a match forward in the matchbook and lit it on the striker without bothering first to tear it free. He snapped his wrist to extinguish the flame and then dropped the matchbook into his pocket. "What's with your faggy neighbor?"

Zach kept walking, cupping his hand around the cigarette as if to protect the glowing tip of it from the night. Raul deliberately bumped into him. "He ever, you know, come on to you or something?"

"Raul!" Zach punched him in the shoulder and then tried to push him into the bushes. "He's a good guy. He wouldn't do that."

Raul laughed, escaped under Zach's arms, and flicked his ash toward the bushes. "Okay, here's a joke, Zachy. A rabbi, a priest, and a lawyer were on an airplane with a bunch of Boy Scouts. One engine caught fire and the other started stalling. The lawyer said, 'We gotta get out of here now, man. There are only three parachutes; I think we should take them.' The rabbi glanced back toward the back of the plane and said, 'But what about the Boy Scouts?' The lawyer says, 'Fuck the Boy Scouts!' 'Oh,' says the priest, 'do you think we have time?'"

Zach punched his friend in the arm. "Screw you, Raul."

"Oh, Zach, do you think we have time?"

At the base of the University Bridge Raul dropped down from the bike path to the abandoned railroad bed, knelt in the gravel, and picked up six or seven rocks the size of his fist. "For the bridge." He motioned toward the hulk of orange steel looming above them, the freshly painted blue of its trim showing only in small circles illuminated by the streetlights lining the sidewalk. Zach picked up rocks also, filling both his jacket pockets, and then they climbed the embankment up to the bridge and stepped over the guardrail onto the pedestrian walkway.

They walked across the orange metal grill until they came to the center of the drawbridge, stepping carefully over the jagged line where the two sections of sidewalk and road came together. From here they could look east down the canal to the brightly lit buildings of the university, or to the west, across Lake Union, toward the greasy black spires of Gasworks Park. Raul took a rock from his pocket and dropped it from the upper rail, counting off the seconds until they heard it splash below. "One second per three feet," he said. "One hundred twenty feet to the water."

Zach dropped one of his rocks and counted also. "Only ninety. Yours must have landed in a hole." They took turns dropping the rocks and counting, and then had a contest to see who could throw a rock the farthest. Zach probably won, but they really couldn't see the rocks land in the dark. Cars roared by behind them, their tires humming a high-pitched whine across the grill, broken only by the deeper rumble where they crossed the drawbridge joints. The wind blew hard out here on the bridge, but still felt warm against their faces. Zach stood on tiptoe and leaned out against the railing, trying to aim a stone at the red drawbridge light that marked the center of the bridge for boats, and which was protected from Zach's and other boys' intentions by a simple wire cage encircling the bulb. "My mothers are gay too, you know."

"Which mother?"

"Both of them!"

Raul burst out laughing. "What a family!"

"Yeah. . . . They treated you bad though."

"It's okay, Zach. It's because you're still just a kid. They're just trying to keep you out of trouble."

"I'm not a kid!"

"Okay! You're not."

"Josiah would never come on to me. He's not like that at all. He acts more like . . . well, kind of like a femmy father."

"He have a boyfriend or something?"

"He brings guys home with him sometimes."

"No shit! You ever see them do it?"

"Raul!"

"I was just asking."

Zach grabbed Raul's shoulders and began to wrestle him against the rail of the bridge. Raul butted him in the chest with his head and then tried to raise his arms up, breaking the grip, but Zach was stronger than he was and he wrestled Raul's back against the railing and then pretended he was going to throw him off. "Want to go swimming? Nice night for a swim."

Raul laughed and broke his grip and then tried to pick Zach up by the waist. Above them the bridge tender shone a flashlight down on them from his window. "Hey, you boys! Stop that and move on!"

Raul straightened, punching Zach on the shoulder, and then raised his right hand toward the old man, his middle finger in the air. "Get a life, dickless!"

VI

Zach turned the "Closed" sign around at five-thirty and began to sweep the floor in the store while Mr. Shelby disappeared into his bedroom to prepare for his evening bath. The old man said he felt safer having somebody near; he wasn't getting any younger and what if he slipped in the tub when no one was around to hear?

Sometimes, when Mr. Shelby wasn't around, or when he was back in his bedroom or in the storeroom checking inventory, Zach would close his eyes and move about the store trying to imagine the world the old man lived in. Now he finished sweeping and set the broom in its place behind the counter, then entered the bathroom with his eyes squeezed shut, imagining this room as the old man knew it. The cold, stainless steel handrails and towel racks felt icy and white against his fingers, and he noticed for the first time the differences in texture between the unpainted window sills and the slicker surface of the painted bathroom door. The painted door was cooler even, its surface one dimensional and latexed flat. The window wood felt warm and textured, smooth from fine sanding, but still it was possible to feel the individual grain of the wood.

From the door to the sink to the window to the bathtub, Zach could circle the room with three steps and a turn. The sink was higher than most sinks and deeper, its fat round bottom icy and rough under his touch. Zach squinted his eyes, cheating just a little, and he noticed for the first time the odd detail that even a blind man had a mirror above his bathroom sink.

"Zach." The old man stepped into the kitchen and called softly, waiting to place the boy by the sound of his voice.

"I'm in here, Mr. Shelby." Zach glanced one last time in the small round mirror, then turned and knelt down to reach the faucets for the tub. The room steamed quickly, fogging the mirror and tiny window, and laying a fine mist on stainless steel, wood, and porcelain. Zach placed a fresh towel and washcloth on the towel rack at the foot of the tub, then pushed the rack closer so the old man would be able to reach them.

Mr. Shelby sat at the kitchen table, rocking slightly to the sound of his radio. His head tilted slightly ahead of the rest of him, as if his face were rocking and his body just followed. Zach turned off the tub, dried his hands across his pants legs then walked out to the kitchen to stand by Mr. Shelby's chair. "It's ready."

The old man sighed loudly, then raised his arm for Zach to help him stand up. "You're a good boy, Zach," he said sadly. "I know you are. A good boy."

When Mr. Shelby finished his bath he yelled for Zach to help him, and Zach walked slowly back through the curtain, listening to the voice so pleading and shrill. He stood in the kitchen staring through the open bathroom doorway until the old man called his name again. "I'm right here," the boy answered.

Mr. Shelby sat in the grayish, soap-flecked water with his pale white legs stretched out before him and his scrawny chicken back to the door. "Zach? Could you . . ." The old man reached out with his hand until it brushed Zach's shirt front, then grasped it, leaving the damp darkened print from his hand.

"Mr. Shelby . . . I," Zach stopped and touched his wrist. The old man was crying. He cried almost silently with his eyes squinched shut like a child—as if he could have seen through them if he tried, but he didn't.

"You're a good boy, Zach. I know that." The old man's voice was soft, almost imperceptible; Zach pulled back once, then relented and knelt down close to the side of the tub.

While the old man dressed alone in his bedroom, Zach sat on the high stool behind the back counter and stared out through the plate-glass front door. His shirt front was damp and wrinkled, his blue jeans soaked on one thigh where the water from the tub had splashed him. In his head he had a story and he began to make that story rhyme; it was restful to him somehow—to chant to himself that rhyming story. One day he would exhale the story; it would simply exhale from him like a breath. And when he breathed in once again, the story would be gone from him, would be someone else's story which he had simply released through his mouth.

The old man pushed open the curtain and took one step toward the back of the counter. He was dressed in cotton pajamas, a flannel bathrobe, and worn leather slippers over bony white feet. "Zach?" He held out a paper bag with magazines in it, his hand floating patiently in the perennial darkness while he waited for the boy to find it. Zach reached slowly for the package, feeling the old man's dry fingers rest lightly on the inside of his wrist. Zach took the package and wiped his wrist against his hip, trying to erase through rough denim the memory of that papery touch. "I gotta go now."

"You're a good boy, Zach. I know. A good boy."

There was a story the boy meant to tell but he lost it now inside the chanting which began slow and steady in the back of his head. He would think of the story again tomorrow, or he would tell it to Raul when they met that afternoon.

"Please . . ." The old man's voice cut through him.

Zach stared across the dimly lit store, through the glass front door before him. A metro bus pulled up, wheezed exhaust into the side of the building, and its front door opened, expelling half a dozen riders. They milled about for a moment, sorting themselves slowly before heading off in all directions.

"Zach? Are you still here, Zach?" The old man's voice seemed even sadder.

The boy jumped down from the stool, took a Mars bar off the candy rack and drifted toward the front door without speaking. Outside he joined the throng of commuters, unwrapped his chocolate bar, and ate it slowly while walking down Fremont.

Zach walked home slowly, promising himself that he wouldn't return to the old man's store. At home he called out for Josiah or Dagg, his mom, or someone, but, finding himself alone there, relocked the front door and then the door to his bedroom. He sat on his bed with his magazines, letting the photographs the old man slipped him slide out from behind the magazine covers.

Zach looked at each picture carefully, as if trying to memorize every detail. He lay facedown across his bed, grinding his hips against his pillow, but slowly, casually, as if it didn't count, this thing that he did, it didn't count if it happened without his attention, without his thinking.

The pictures this time were old ones—a woman with a large dog; a woman tied with black leather straps to a couch—Zach felt vaguely nauseous and horrified, but reached for himself anyway, stroking himself to orgasm while curled up in a ball on his bed. He came staring at the creepy pictures, then relaxed across his bed. "Pervert," he whispered, still holding his limp penis. "Old fucking pervert. You can't even see them."

Zach had nightmares that night and woke himself yelling from dreams he couldn't quite recall. He sat up with his back against the wall, covering himself with more blankets, and waited patiently for morning. Some nights lately when he couldn't sleep, he would crawl out his bedroom window and across the roof to Josiah's living room window, where, if Josiah was alone and not sleeping, he would let Zach in and they would watch old movies together, sometimes until dawn. Mornings he wasn't in his own bed Patrice or Dagg would come and get him and walk him, still half asleep, back into his own bed, where once it was light outside he could sleep soundly into the afternoon.

"Zach? What is it?" They'd finally stopped asking, because he would always look away and down as if he lacked the words to say it.

"He needs a father," Patrice would repeat. "A woman can't teach a boy to be a man."

"He's got Josiah."

"Not Josiah. He needs . . ."

"We all need fathers, but who do you know who gets one?"

"He needs a real father. He needs . . ."

"He needs . . ."

What did he need? Not even Zach would be able to say.

VII

On Friday Zach slept late, waking only at noon, long after Patrice and Dagg were gone from the house. He dressed for work, ate breakfast, then walked slowly toward Shelby's store, arriving exactly at two. But once his hand touched the door handle, some part of him refused to go in.

Zach released his hold on the door, watching through the glass as Mr. Shelby sat quietly behind the counter, perhaps waiting for the door to open. Instead, Zach walked up to 45th and caught a bus to the University District. On the Avenue he walked and hung out, ate Chinese food, then strolled onto the university campus and joined some guys playing hacky sack in the grass beside the fountain. When he got home after dark, Patrice, Dagg, and Josiah were waiting for him in the living room, sitting together on the couch.

"Zach, we want to talk to you." Dagg brushed at her thighs nervously and then stood up.

Zach's breathing shifted and grew shallow. He stared from one to the other, but their faces were unreadable. "What?" he said finally, edging closer into the room.

Dagg nodded to Patrice, who elbowed Josiah. But Josiah edged away from her. "He's your kid, Patrice."

Patrice straightened her skirt. "You're thirteen," she said.

"Yes, I know that." Zach backed farther toward the bedroom.

Josiah snorted and Dagg put one hand over her eyes. "Good start, Patrice. Tell him his name next."

"Zach," Patrice almost shouted. "Why weren't you at work today?"

Zach felt something in his chest snap tight, as if something inside him just closed up forever. "I didn't do anything," he mumbled.

"I stopped in to see you."

"Let me alone." Zach could feel something edging through his chest like panic.

Dagg stood up and walked to the dining room table, then picked up a magazine and a stack of photographs. "I was cleaning your room. I found these—"

Zach tried to bolt past her, but Josiah stopped him. "People can talk about sex. It doesn't have to be a secret."

"I didn't *do anything*!"

"Great," Dagg said. "Let's make him defensive."

The chicken Patrice was frying on the stove crackled in the hot oil, and Patrice walked back into the kitchen to turn it. "That's right,

Zach," she yelled from the doorway. "It's your life. It's your business. We shouldn't have . . . brought it up. We shouldn't . . . interfere in your life."

Zach glared at the floor, bunching and unbunching his hands in his jeans pockets. He didn't know whether to hit someone or cry.

"Zach, is there . . ." Dagg stopped, looking helplessly at Josiah.

"Zach," Josiah tried softly. "Sex, you know, and all that. How bodies go through changes. It can be . . . confusing sometimes. We just want you to know. It doesn't have to be a mystery. You can . . . you know . . . ask questions. You can talk to us about sex."

"Leave me alone." Zach tried to push past them to flee into his room.

"Zach, about those pictures . . ." Josiah walked to the window before turning to face the boy again. "You know, those women in them . . . it looks as if they're getting hurt. . . . It's okay to like sexual pictures—to like to look at them, I mean. But those photographs looked real. Those women in them. Those things that happened to them hurt them."

"You can't just go in my room. Stay out of it!"

Dagg stood awkwardly in the doorway to the kitchen. "I went to change your sheets. . . . It's Friday. I always change your sheets on Friday. Those magazines . . . I don't understand about those pictures."

Zach stared down at the floor, waiting patiently as if she might get bored and just go away.

"Sexual things can be confusing." Josiah tried to smile a little and opened his hands. "Maybe if you want to talk to a guy about things . . ."

"You think I'm gonna talk about sex with a fag? Get real!" Zach punched the door frame to his bedroom and rested his head against the wall. He felt ashamed to turn and look at Josiah.

Josiah turned back into the living room. "You don't have to talk to anyone, Zach . . . but those pictures you're keeping . . . you're going to have to explain them to at least yourself some day."

"Are you going to call other people names every time you're hurting?" Dagg sat down at the dining room table and stared at the boy.

"Leave me alone! I'm not . . . at least I'm not . . ." Zach stopped, suddenly aware that he was hurting Josiah. He didn't want to hurt

Josiah, he just wanted to breathe. "Fuck this," he said shortly and stomped into his bedroom. Before any of them would think to follow, he crawled out over the roof, into Josiah's bedroom window, grabbed a jeans jacket from Josiah's closet, and fled down the stairs.

Dagg finally found him just after midnight, sitting alone in Daylight Donuts. She tapped softly on the glass to get his attention and then came inside and slid onto a stool beside him. "I'm sorry," she said quietly. "I don't think we quite handled that right."

The boy nodded but wouldn't look up. He stared down at the counter as if he could somehow read his fortune in the tiny gray swirls that danced across the faded red Formica counter.

"After you left . . . your mom went over the roof trying to find you. She left the chicken frying on the stove and the kitchen caught on fire."

Zach looked up at her with surprise. "Did the house burn down?"

Dagg shook her head. "Josiah had a fire extinguisher."

For some reason her saying this made Zach laugh. "I'm sorry too," he said finally. "I'm sorry I called Josiah a fag." He looked down, sad again, and what the laughter had opened, completely snapped shut.

"Let's go home."

"I'm not going." Zach held his mug out for the waitress to refill it.

"Of course you're going home!" Dagg waved away an offer of coffee. "You're thirteen years old, for chrissakes. You shouldn't even be drinking coffee."

The waitress wiped the counter in front of Dagg. "Want anything?"

"Zach? You want a doughnut?" Dagg ordered them each a chocolate iced doughnut, and a cup of coffee for herself. They ate in silence until the doughnuts were gone, then Dagg drained her mug and turned toward the boy. "Come on. Let's go home now."

Zach shook his head without looking at her. "Raul says I can live with him if I want to."

"Raul? The Puerto Rican hooker?"

"He's not Puerto Rican. . . . He's Mayan."

"Mayan? Zach, you're still a kid. Guys like Raul . . . they're . . . headed for trouble and if you're not careful you'll go with him."

"He's my friend."

"Did he give you those pictures?"

"No." Zach wrapped his hands around his empty mug.

"You ought to pick your friends better. I know what I'm talking about, Zach."

Zach laid a dollar on the counter to pay for his coffee. "You don't know a thing about it."

Outside on the street again, he stuffed his hands into his jacket pockets while Dagg stared helplessly from the boy to the empty street. "I'm sorry about tonight," she tried again. "We wanted to . . . I wanted to . . . help somehow."

"I shouldn't have called Josiah a fag."

"Yeah. You hurt his feelings. I think he felt really bad about that."

Zach nodded and looked down. He'd felt bad too, trapped and scared and somehow dirty, and he felt all that again suddenly, and like he needed to get away just to breathe. "I'll see you."

"Zach."

"I'll call you. I'm come by tomorrow." He walked around the corner and down toward Aurora, his hands in his jacket pockets curled into fists.

Zach found Raul outside of Tower Records sometime just after one in the morning. They walked the ten blocks to the Ridgemont Theater, where Raul unlocked the padlock from the side door and held the door open for Zach to enter. For a moment a security light from the alley illuminated the room in front of him, and Zach could see worn brown carpet, rows of old plush red theater seats, and the gentle downward slope of aisle that led to a dark wood proscenium, and above it, the heavy, plush red curtains that covered the screen. The theater was completely empty, and sound carried through it in an odd echoing way. Raul closed the heavy steel door with a clang, and in the darkness Zach could hear his friend's footsteps leading toward the back of the theater. "This way."

Zach followed the voice up the aisle and through two swinging wood doors into the empty theater lobby. He heard a metallic click of switches, and dim theater lights softly lit the room. The lobby walls were a deep plush red, set off almost to the ceiling with ornate gold sconces from which dim light glowed.

"Here." Raul led the way up wide carpeted steps into the balcony, through two more swinging doors and out onto the balcony itself, where they could look down upon the empty theater. Zach stared down into the theater, feeling the oddness of its silence. Behind him Raul continued up the stairs to the projection room in back.

"This way, come on." Raul's high girlish laugh sounded somewhere above him, and Zach looked up the steep aisle to see the boy standing at a narrow metal door high against the back wall. Raul flicked a switch in the projection booth wall and bright white light poured out of the three small square projection windows.

From the door, one had to climb a narrow metal ladder, like a ship's, up ten rungs to the actual room. The air was stuffy and close, sulphurous, old, and much too lived in. Three giant projectors crouched in the center of things, their large eyes gazing outward through the portals toward the closed curtains, and behind them racks of film canisters leaned against a metal counter above a small pallet bed and a heap of not-very- clean-smelling clothes.

"Home." Raul smiled and flopped down on his pallet, then rose immediately and began fiddling with the huge projectors. "I know how to work these. They're carbon arc projectors, not those computer things the new theaters use. Real flame, that's what you smell. These can cook a stuck piece of film in a second and a half." Raul flicked on one of the monsters, which arced up a hot white light, illuminating a long rectangle onto the curtains below. Raul reached across to a metal breaker box on the wall and threw a bar switch upward, and immediately the theater curtains slid open.

The projector clicked and hummed, filling the air with the stench of hot metal and something sulphurous like rotting eggs. Empty sprockets clicked against their pins and the large rear reel spun freely, taking up nothing. Raul fiddled with an ancient-looking radio resting on the back cabinet, and in a minute the projection room and then the theater were filled with the sound of the Talking Heads singing, "Take me to the river . . ."

Raul danced across the room and placed Zach carefully in an open window. "Watch," he said and then danced to the ladder, descended into the balcony, and was gone.

When he appeared again it was on the thin apron of stage in front of the now-lit screen, barefoot, his shirt off, his tight jeans half open; he danced across the screen, all details washed out in the bright white light, a lithe, thin boy before his own enormous shadow.

"Come on, dance with me!" He motioned for Zach to come down and join him, but Zach stood frozen, staring through the small square window, a little in awe and too scared to move. Raul danced from one end of the stage to the other, his thin sharp face ecstatic, as if he were in love with the feel of his own body. "When you watch people on the screen, they're twenty feet tall," he shouted over the music. "They can't . . . they don't even know you're watching. What if they did? What if they did those things knowing people were watching?"

The song on the radio ended and the station broke for a commercial. "Top knob on the right," Raul yelled. "Turn it down."

Zach turned and prodded a couple of knobs and found the power switch before the volume. A beer commercial thumped an imitation rap beat, and Zach punched the button that turned the whole thing off. On the stage Raul breathed heavily and sat down, swinging his feet above the empty house, a trickle of sweat running from his neck down his bare chest.

"I brought a trick here once. Danced for him and let him do me. Fifty fucking dollars; he was so ecstatic." Raul raised his arms in the white light and tried to make shadow puppets move against the screen. "Ha! You like this, Zach? You're such a kid. Come here, I want to show you something."

He waited while Zach descended into the theater, climbed up on the stage and sat down next to him, looking scared and uncertain. "Look how beautiful we are in the light. See how it was made to show us?" Raul started dancing again, this time without the radio, making a ba-de-bbaa sound that was supposed to pass for song.

"That man, Josiah, has got some ugly legs. How would you like to go through life with legs that ugly?" The boy giggled and pulled Zach to his feet. "Dance with me, Zachy. You ever seen any legs so ugly?"

Zach laughed and pulled back against Raul's hand. He didn't know how to dance, and besides, Raul was starting to scare him a little.

"So ugly I don't ever want to see the rest of him naked."

Zach looked down at his own legs, and then sat back on the apron of the stage. One hand began to work at a hole in the denim covering his knee. His fingers caught under the attached threads and pulled and worked them until they tore out. Raul stopped dancing and stared at his friend's ducked head. "Is he doing you, man? The fucker looks like he's got AIDS or something." Zach's fingers kept working the fabric around his now-visible knee. "Somebody's doing you, aren't they Zach? You're just a kid. Nobody's supposed to be doing a kid."

Zach continued to work the fabric of his pants leg, working and tearing the hole larger and larger. As his fingers worried the frayed-out fabric, his feet banged rhythmically against the side of the stage.

"Is it Josiah?"

Zach shook his head no, still staring at his knees. Finally, in a quiet voice, he said, "Mr. Shelby."

"Shelby?" Raul stopped dancing. "The blind guy? You couldn't fucking stop a blind guy?"

Zach wrapped his arms across his chest and started to cry, at first almost silently, but soon his crying grew louder and he hugged his knees to his chest and began to rock back and forth.

Raul sat down next to him and touched his shaking shoulders. "Oh, Christ. You're such a kid. Stop that now. I'm gonna fix this." He put his arms around his friend and began to rock with him. "Just sit still and let me think, OK?"

VIII

The boys waited the next morning until Dagg and Patrice had both gone to work and then returned to Zach's place and fixed themselves breakfast. Raul added milk and sugar to his coffee and carried it to the couch, where he could sit and look out the window. Zach barely picked at his eggs and toast, nervously watching Raul and then looking away. He felt embarrassed, ashamed that he'd told. Now Raul would think he was a wuss—some wimpy kid who couldn't even fight off a blind guy.

But he hadn't been forced—that was what he couldn't say. It was worse than that; he'd been passive, and wasn't that the same as willing? The old man had seemed so pathetic somehow. Lost and alone with his ridiculous hard-on. Zach had felt responsible for it. And the old man just seemed so pathetic.

"What's his phone number?" Raul put down his coffee and reached for the phone.

"What are you doing?"

"I'm gonna call the son-of-a-bitch. I'm going to tell the bastard that if he bothers you again I'll kill him."

"But—"

"Just give me the number, OK?"

Raul dialed, waited a moment, and then in a fake deep voice began a harangue against the listener. Zach was so intent on his friend's performance that he didn't notice his mom and Dagg standing at the door. Raul finished and hung up, grinning, then noticed the women now in the room.

"What's going on here?" Patrice looked at Zach.

"Nothing!"

"Who was he talking to?"

"Just tell her, Zach."

"No!"

"Tell her!"

"Tell me what?" Patrice set her books on the table and motioned to Dagg, who'd followed her into the room.

Zach grasped both knees and rocked forward.

"Tell me what, Zach? You in trouble? Who was he talking to? Who were you talking to?"

Dagg looked from Zach on the couch to Raul twisting his hands around the curtain covering the window. "What's going on?"

"Tell her!" Raul shouted.

"Nothing!" Zach jumped up and tried to run out.

"Hold on." Dagg stopped him.

Raul stepped forward, letting go of the curtain. "Tell her, Zach."

"No!"

"The blind guy he works for."

"Raul, don't say it!" Zach grabbed at his arm.

Raul shrugged free and looked at Patrice. "He's been, you know, messing with Zach."

"Messing?" Patrice looked momentarily lost. She glanced from Raul to Zach, and then back to Dagg. "Sexually, you mean?" Her hand tightened on the back of Dagg's shirt.

Raul nodded and then looked down. "I just thought, you know. Nobody ought to mess with a kid." He glanced back at Zach, but the boy turned away.

"I hate you, Raul. You ruined my whole life!"

Raul ducked his head and took a step toward the door. "I guess I'll be taking off. I'll see you around, Zach." His face quivered like a child's for a moment before he caught himself and froze it in place.

IX

From his bed Zach could hear his mom, Dagg, and Josiah in the living room talking, their voices humming together like the buzzing of flies. That night he dreamed they were all in separate rowboats floating down a river, and ahead he could see the water drop dangerously through a series of falls. His mother's boat flipped and went over the rapids, and Dagg's spun dangerously out of control. Zach tried to steer close in along the shore, but the falls grew louder and louder and the water ripped and tugged at him, pulling him into the faster, swirling, middle current.

His own screams woke him as he bolted upright in bed, his body sweat drenched and starting to shiver.

"Zach, wake up." Patrice came into his bedroom and sat down on the edge of his bed, smoothing the blankets across his legs. "It was a dream. A bad dream."

"I don't want my paws to get wet!"

"It was a dream, honey."

"My paws. I want to keep my paws dry, but they keep getting slimy and wet." Zach held his hands before him, moving them slowly up and down like flippers. "I wanted to keep them dry," he said sadly, now fully awake and back in the present. "But they kept on getting slimy and wet."

Patrice took his cold damp hands between her palms and rubbed them. "It was a dream, baby. Just a dream. I'll sit here until you go back to sleep."

Zach tensed slightly and balled up his fingers. "I'm not going to sleep. I don't want to."

"It's OK, Zach. I'll sit here. I'll sit here until the sun comes up, or until you sleep, whichever comes first."

"If you tell anybody, I'll have to go to jail forever." Zach hunched over his knees and hugged them through the blankets and covers.

"No. You won't. Who told you that?"

"Mr. Shelby said it. He said it was my fault." Zach picked at his wool blanket, running the soft satiny edge between his hands. "I don't want to go to jail!" He started rocking again and began to cry.

Patrice lay down next to him and began crying with him. "I don't know what the right thing is to do. I don't know the right thing. Dagg and Josiah say we have to call the police."

"Please no!"

"I don't know. I try to know but I don't know!" Patrice buried her head in the pillow, her own cries now louder than Zach's.

Dagg came into the room and knelt down next to them, trying to hold them both at once in her arms. "We have to tell, Zach. And not just for you. Men who do things like that—he'll find other boys—it isn't just you."

They were met at the Wallingford Police Station by Maya Lantry from Seattle Rape Crisis. She was a large, sloppily dressed black woman with nappy red-brown hair and run-down-in-the-heel loafers that seemed too large for her feet. She greeted Josiah with a hug and then turned her gaze to Zach, taking him in with a glance at once searing, sympathetic, and sad. "My name's Maya, Zach. I'm here as your advocate. Do you know about that?"

Zach stared at her suspiciously, not really knowing why she was there. Only Josiah had said she was an old friend, and the police, he said, could be such idiots. She didn't wait for the boy's reply but, like a woman who knows her job in its most minute and careful timing, turned and steered them into the police station, explaining to Zach what he could expect. "Are you his mother?" She reached out and gently touched Dagg's shoulder.

"His mother's not here. I'm her partner."

Maya glanced quickly at Josiah, who met her questioning look with a shrug. "She was going to come," Dagg continued. "We decided to do this. But when we got to the station she wouldn't come in."

She looked at Maya expectantly, as if hoping for some explanation, but Maya had turned her attention to Zach. "The investigator will ask you more questions. If you don't like a question, just say so and you don't have to answer. Sometimes they ask you stupid questions. That's my job, Zach, to help you remember to take care of yourself. OK? OK?" she said again, turning the boy so they looked eye to eye.

Zach nodded his head slowly. It had suddenly become clear to him that she wouldn't stop staring until he answered.

The detective filled out forms in triplicate while Zach slowly told him what had happened, and then answered and re-answered the same dozen questions.

"What's going to happen to him?" Zach asked the cop who was typing the complaint.

"We'll try to lock the scumbag up if we can."

Zach wrapped his arms around his knees and began rocking. "He's just an old guy," he said. "I didn't tell him to stop or nothing. I didn't tell him nothing. . . . I could've made him stop."

"It's not your fault. You're a kid. He's a grown-up." Maya leaned forward in her seat, trying to catch Zach's eye, but he turned away from her, from all of them, wondering if he had to like her.

"Men like that prey on children."

Zach bunched his hands in his pockets and stared at his feet. "You don't know him. You don't know a thing about it."

When the police arrested Mr. Shelby, the old man began to cry. He denied everything and wouldn't stop crying. Zach had to pick him out of a police lineup; one weeping white-haired blind man among five sighted strangers.

"He didn't hurt me," Zach kept saying. To the police, the assistant district attorney, the woman from Rape Crisis. "It's not like he hurt me. He's just sad, a sad old guy who can't see."

Dagg kept repeating she was going to kill him, but after the lineup she too sat cold and numb in the police station, while Zach answered the same questions one more time.

They wanted Zach to go to the hospital, though there were no wounds or scars to check for—something about the investigation and how they could use that at the trial. The emergency room was loud and bright and smelled like a mixture of antiseptic, floor cleaner, blood, old pee, and fear. While they waited to be seen, two young men who'd been cut up in a knife fight came in. They sat across the narrow hall from Zach, trying to hold their cut stomachs closed with their hands, but the blood still leaked past them and dripped onto the floor. Zach tried not to look at them and huddled between Josiah and Dagg, but as each droplet landed he flinched again and tightened. The blood made the room smell hot and animal, like a den in which something filthy had happened.

Finally a nurse led them to an examination table surrounded by splattered white curtains and illuminated by two shrill blue reflector lamps that hung over the table on long cords. The physician's assistant, a colorless woman with limp brown hair, a tight mouth, and a stained pink smock, was cool and efficient, saying all the worst things with a kind of calculated horror. "Results for syphilis and gonorrhea we'll have in about a week. As for HIV infection, he might test negative right now but there's no way of telling for certain for another six months. Bring him back in six months and we'll test again, but even then we can't be certain."

"He's thirteen," Josiah said, as if unable to believe the woman could feel so little.

She shrugged at Josiah, pursing her thin lips in a show of distaste. "Things happen," she said finally, turning her back on them to wash her hands at the stainless steel sink.

Outside in the car Patrice raised her hands toward Zach as if wanting to hug him, but he shrugged her touch off and stared out the window. "I'm sorry, Zach. I couldn't face it. I couldn't make myself go in there."

"What did you think would happen, Patrice?" Dagg pulled out of the parking lot, not looking at her either.

"I thought they would . . . put me in jail . . . or take Zach away. They would know I've been a terrible mother." She tried to stroke Zach's arm again, but he pulled away from her, finding some solace in the place inside him that turned chanting into shrill white noise. There was a place in his head he had learned to go to. Nothing existed there but the noise and the vibration—it was a tunnel kind of place, and when memories went in it they got lost inside the white noise and finally disappeared.

In the days that followed, Patrice vacillated between trying to comfort Zach and being tense and afraid because they'd called the police. "They'll think I'm a bad mother," she kept insisting to Dagg. "They'll take Zach away because I'm a bad mother."

While Dagg, Josiah, and Zach had moved into some kind of state of emergency, Patrice tried to continue as if nothing had changed. She would comfort Zach in a vague sort of way and then become distracted, forgetting her words in midsentence. She seemed stunned and confused by the way Zach had fallen apart, suddenly having nightmares and crying in his sleep. It was because they had called the police, she insisted. He had, after all, functioned fine all summer without telling; why else would he fall apart like this all at once?

Fall quarter classes began again in late September, and Patrice signed up for eighteen credits. She left the apartment before eight most mornings and didn't get home until after eleven at night. Weekends she spent in the library trying to catch up on all her course work. When she did see Zach, she would flutter about him so distractedly that he began to resent her presence even more than the time she was gone, and in those moments when she became suddenly guilt-ridden and wanted to try to be what she thought was a good mother, Zach shrugged off her attentions and hid in his room.

Five weeks into the semester Patrice began packing to go on a geology class field trip in spite of Zach's almost constant nightmares. Dagg and Josiah argued and yelled and tried to talk her out of it, but Patrice kept saying it was like a job—she got paid to go to school and she couldn't take the state's money and not go on the field trips.

"Since when did you care about giving the state fair value for its money? You've been hustling school grants since the day I met you." Dagg shoved the duffel bag out of their bedroom and into the hall.

"Leave it!" Patrice straightened the bag and continued packing, filling it with a sleeping bag, clothing, and packages of instant soup.

Zach watched them from his place on the bed, feeling the coolness of the wall though his thin T-shirt. "I don't care if she goes or not, Dagg."

"You can miss this one thing. Zach needs you here. I do!" Dagg caught Patrice's wrist above the duffel, stopping the hand's downward flight into the bag.

Patrice shrugged free and continued packing, no longer looking at Dagg as she spoke. "I've been trying to get somewhere . . . you know . . . to make Zach a life . . . someplace out of this place . . . where . . ."

"Where what, Patrice? You think there's a place you can take him where this won't have happened?"

"If we didn't live in such a—" Patrice motioned around the bedroom with a rolled T-shirt in her hand.

Dagg stared at Patrice across the open half-filled duffel. "You think this wouldn't have happened to Zach if we had money? Is that the thing you've decided to say?"

"He wouldn't have taken that old creep's job, for one thing!"

"You wanted him to work there. Don't you remember? You were almost ecstatic."

"Don't say that!"

"It's true. Ask Josiah. It had something to do with *Red River* and a real manly man or something."

"You!" Patrice stuffed a jacket into the top of the pack and then squeezed the canvas tight in order to zip it. She yanked the zipper closed while Dagg got up, walked into the bathroom, and returned with Patrice's blow dryer, which she threw onto the half-closed duffel.

"Don't forget this. You might need it where you're going."

"What do you think I'm trying to do?"

"Go have sex with strangers and forget about it. Isn't that how you deal with your pain? You throw down with some yahoo you just met today."

"How dare you!"

"I've always known you mess around. You want to sleep with strangers, fine. But don't pretend you're going camping and get all righteous about your kid's needs—you've been an ice queen ever since he got hurt."

"He didn't get hurt." Patrice closed the duffel bag completely and lugged it toward the door. "He sucked some old man's dick. Haven't you? Haven't I? Doesn't everybody?"

Patrice didn't return when the field trip was over, and they still had not heard from her a week later. Dagg finally called the school, only to discover that Patrice hadn't been seen there in over a month.

A month. The longest month. Summer had ended in the middle of it and Zach had started ninth grade. Josiah had gotten the flu sometime within it and the sickness dragged on, week after week. Most nights the nightmares still flooded Zach, and he sat quietly in the darkness, his back pressed to the cool plaster wall. It was as if all summer he had kept those things from surfacing, but once loosened and acknowledged they would not stop tormenting him.

He'd not seen Raul since the morning Raul had squealed to Dagg and his mother. It still felt like betrayal, or worse yet: Raul probably thought that Zach was a girl. He could not protect himself from a blind guy; Zach shook his head deliberately, as if trying to shake loose the memory of his own confusion and arousal, denying the old man's wheedling need.

Zach went to school each morning and stayed away from home until dinnertime each night. He grew silent and more distant; his inner world could no longer be shared. Sometimes after dinner Josiah would ask if he wanted to play Risk again, but Risk felt like childhood now, like something he was losing, and some long-ago sadness the boy needed to flee. Zach loved Josiah and he loved Dagg too, though he hoped no one would make him say it. But he was leaving them—slowly, imperceptibly, day after day, he was wandering into places that neither would ever be able to follow.

Dagg

I

Nine-year-old Dagger sat on a bench in the sun outside Valencia's General Store eating red licorice and watching a thin dark-haired woman set sculptures out on the front porch of the art gallery across the road. The woman noticed the lanky, unkempt girl watching her, and waved a sort of tentative wave, perhaps surprised by any unfamiliar child in a village as small as Galisteo, New Mexico.

Encouraged by the wave, Dagger crossed the dirt road and stared up into the gallery window. Inside, old Punch and Judy marionettes hung awkwardly from their crossbars, and Dagger wanted to climb the porch steps to see them. She waited patiently a moment, hoping the woman would invite her, but now that Dagger was at the base of the porch steps the woman turned away from her and began to sweep around the heavy wood sculptures she had dragged onto the porch.

"That's an old Punch you got there," Dagger said finally.

The woman stopped her work and stared down at her. "You like marionettes?"

Dagger shook her head no. "They scare me," she whispered.

"They're not real. They won't hurt you." The gallery lady seemed somehow annoyed by Dagger's fear.

Dagger drew a line in the dirt with the edge of her shoe. "I know how to work them, though. My dad taught me."

The woman looked distracted. "Shouldn't you be in school or something?"

"Well, yeah, I guess so." Dagger looked up and down the street. "But, you know."

"What?"

"Those kids at school all know each other, and nobody knows me."

"Somebody must know you," the woman said. She turned her back on Dagger and began to sweep the porch clear of dust and fallen leaves from the overhanging cottonwood. Dagger took a step backward, responding physically to an unacknowledged feeling that she was the thing the woman wanted to sweep clear.

"My dad, I guess. My dad knows me. And the circus people. If we ever stayed with one, I mean. Which we don't, because of my dad's bad eye."

"The circus," the woman said. "You're with the circus?"

"Carnival now. Used to be the circus till my dad lost his eye."

"What's your name?" The woman stopped her broom for an instant but kept it cocked in the air between them.

"Dagger."

"Dagger what?"

"Yeah. Dagger What."

"That's a funny name."

Dagger looked down at the dirt between her sneakers. "I swallow swords," she said. "Well, no. Long knives, really. The taller you grow then the more you can swallow."

"Where's your mom while you're doing that?"

Dagger glanced back over her shoulder toward Valencia's as if expecting her mother would suddenly appear. After waiting a moment in seeming expectation, she dropped her head and began to chew ferociously on her lower lip before finally looking up at the stranger. "My mom disappeared with a rabbit."

"Women don't disappear with rabbits!"

Dagger unclenched her hands inside her jeans pockets and raised her shoulders in a theatrical shrug. "The rabbit's owner was a magician."

The woman looked embarrassed by that piece of information. "Where's your dad?"

"He ballys mostly, calling for the sideshows. He used to be a catcher with a trapeze troupe, but like I said, he lost an eye." Dagger climbed to the top step and grasped the rough wood rail with one hand. Then she reached upward with her other hand and locked the two over the bar as if she would physically resist any attempt to make her go.

The woman brushed her hair off her face and made a motion with her broom again. "I'd better get back to work."

Dagger opened one hand above the railing and stared into her open palm. "About that Punch," she said. "You'd better oughta watch him. Sometimes he does terrible things."

The woman followed her stare toward the puppet in the blue-framed window. "What's wrong with him?" she asked finally.

"Nothing's wrong exactly. He's made to be bad." Dagger grinned up at her. "You're scared of him, I bet. You'd better be!" She released her grasp from the handrail and walked over to the showroom window, resting her forehead against the glass and letting one finger trace the outline of the puppet hanging from the sill. An old Punch, his hand-carved lips were chipped in spots but still shrill red and leering; his maniacal carved eyes still showed flakes of brilliant blue. "Punch is *evil*," Dagger said suddenly, drawing out the word. "People act like he's for children, but he's not."

"How do you know?"

"I know about Punch," Dagger said. "I know *all* about him. They used to have Punch in the carnivals—the old ones in the Middle Ages."

The woman waved her hand before her face as if she were trying to wave Dagger back down the stairs, and Dagger straightened in response, pressing close into the gallery window and laying her palms flat against the glass.

Finally the woman sighed loudly and walked to the other side of the porch. "I'd better open up now. The tourists will be coming soon."

"You don't even want to mention Judy." Dagger returned to the steps again and draped her arms around the handrail.

"What?"

"How come Punch always beats her up and throws the baby out the window?"

"What did you say?"

"Out the window!"

The woman took a step forward again and waved toward Dagger with a half-opened hand. "You live in Galisteo?"

"There." The child pointed out into the Galisteo basin. "My dad and me have a trailer in the basin. You can see it if you follow the river. It's about three miles from town."

"Did you walk here?"

"I was on my way to school, but I got . . . mis-started. Is that a word? Mis-started?"

"You're supposed to go to school, you know. It's the law, for one thing."

"Yeah. I know it. But we move around a lot, and my dad, he says it's my prerogative."

The woman laughed. "Where'd you learn a word like that?"

"Punch taught me, maybe. You know he's evil."

"Why do you want to make him scary?"

"I don't make him scary; he *is* scary." Dagger swung out over the railing, then glanced over her shoulder toward the marionettes.

"He's just a wooden toy to me," the woman said impatiently. "Now if you'll excuse me, I have to—"

"I know," Dagger said. "Punch told me. He whispers things about you. Then the people in the village hear them."

"You'd better run along now, before Punch tells me about *you*."

Dagger swung out from the side of the steps, then released her grip and jumped backward, landing in a flower bed. "He knows about my dad, mostly. Mostly he knows about my dad."

The woman folded her arms across her chest and leaned against the door frame, and Dagger had the distinct feeling she wanted her to go away now. The wind gusted up hard and a dust devil whirled up on the road beside her. Dagger covered her mouth with her jacket and slouched down against the steps again. "I hate it when the wind blows. In the basin, out there, all month it's been blowing. The trailer rocks and the windows scream. It hurts my ears when the wind blows. My dad hates it too, and drinks more. In the spring here I get scared, a little." She said the words hurriedly, as if she could disown them before they came out. But the woman turned away in the middle of a sentence and began to pull shut the heavy blue wood shutters that closed off the gallery windows.

"Batten down the hatches," Dagger whispered.

"What?"

"That's what my dad says. Batten down the hatches! There's a squall coming."

"How long do you stay in Galisteo?"

"We hook up with the show in spring." While speaking Dagger ran one dirty hand along the railing, stroking it gently as if she were petting something soft.

"You must like to travel." The woman seemed relieved to hear she'd soon be going, and even smiled at Dagger a little.

"It's better on the road. My dad . . . there's more people around and he . . . well mostly he's different."

"Does he hit you?" The woman looked shaken by her own question. She turned away from Dagger and began to move the sculptures toward the back of the porch.

"Like Punch," Dagger said slowly, "sometimes he's evil." She stretched, released the handrail and stood up, taking a tentative step toward the road. "In the spring, last year at school—" Dagger glanced over her shoulder, then stopped again. "We were learning about carrying. You know, how they do that, like when they carry the two? Well, we were learning about that one day and then I had to leave again. We hooked up with a tent show in April, but I wondered about that two sometimes. Like where they carry it. I felt bad I never learned where they carry that two."

"The circus," the woman looked relieved. "I thought you said carnival."

"Yeah," Dagger said. "Midway. My dad and me do midway shows."

"What did you say your dad does?"

Dagger kicked at the dirt again and then rocked out on the edges of her sneakers. "Sideshow stuff. You know. He ballys: *Step right up. Only one thin dollar! See the tattooed woman! Every inch tells a tale! See the flame-eating girl and the wild pigs of Borneo! Fun and entertainment for the entire family!!!*"

"You do that good."

"Yeah." Dagger sat back on the bottom step and stared at her sneakers. "About that two," she said. "Everybody at school knows where they carry it by now."

The woman shifted the last sculpture and stared down at Dagg, then descended the two wooden steps and sat down beside her. "What's your name, really? It's not really Dagger."

Dagger shoved her hands into her pockets and looked away down the road. At the edge of town she could see the Spanish Catholic church where the old priest in his torn work shirt bent working in the garden.

"Julius. Orange Julius," she said finally.

"What?" The woman looked annoyed again.

"That's what my dad calls me, sometimes. Julius, Orange Julius."

"Does he?" The woman stopped and stared down at Dagg. Then, shaking her head, she asked, "How old are you?"

"Turned nine in February."

"You'll be grown." The woman paused. "You'll meet someone. A boy or something." She looked confused and sad again, and Dagger got the feeling she wanted her to disappear.

II

The wind howled a low moan across the western edge of the Galisteo basin, and from her bed inside the narrow trailer Dagger could hear the gusts begin somewhere far off on the edge of the basin and then rise and swell across the flatlands, roaring like a freight train past her, rattling the windows, and shaking the thin metallic shell until the cheap wood-paneled walls shivered from its passing. The bed shook slightly and Dagger pulled the covers higher and listened for the next gust's distant beginning.

In the front of the trailer, beyond the faded cotton print curtain her father had hung to give the appearance of privacy, he sat slumped at the narrow Formica foldaway table, drinking Wild Turkey from a water tumbler and shuddering slightly at the passing of each new howling blast.

The wind-driven nights had always been the worst ones, and here, in the sink pan of the empty windswept basin, the wind was constant and unrelenting from the early March thaw until late May. The desert held no spring beyond this—no gentle budding up of daffodils, no warm April rains. The *Third Grade Reader*'s stories about Glenn and Annie described a different kind of springtime, and it was the bitter contrast between the book's description of April's budding sweetness and the bitter wind of a desert spring day that first led Dagger to suspect that her school books might lie.

The wind shook and tore at the trailer walls, spraying the aluminum shell with a lashing of sand. Dagger could taste the dust-filled wind now; it seeped microscopically through window seams and door cracks, depositing a layer of fine dust on everything it touched. Dagger reached above her head, tightening the crank on the roll-out slat windows, then stretched almost to the foot of the bed to reach the crank windows on the trailer's back wall.

On the other side of the curtain a metal-legged chair scraped across linoleum; Dagger's father walked the two steps to the kitchen counter and poured himself another shot. Dagger held her breath, listening, until he stepped back again and sank into the vinyl kitchen chair, which wheezed perceptibly as his weight settled in. She had learned more than once these past years to listen with one ear to the night noises and the other to her father, and so was able now without being conscious of it to separate the wild rush of the windstorm from the subtle telling noises that marked her father's moods and intentions and determined his plans for the rest of the night. Three short drinks from a water tumbler, and if he rose then and moved out of hearing into the bathroom, then checked the door and dimmed the lights, things would be OK for that night. But if he poured himself another drink, a more common occurrence when the weather was terrible, Dagger would hold her breath and listen for the moment his footsteps would stumble toward her, for the moment the cotton curtain pulled back.

When she was four and the visits began, she could make so little sense of them that she believed in the night that she was smothered by a monster. Each night the monster had come, she was convinced further of its nocturnal reality by the hot denlike funk it carried with it and the animal musk it left damp and cold on the sheets. By eight, she had forgotten the monster and found instead the numbers, the story of numbers she kept in her head. She would listen for the liquid gurgle of the whiskey being poured a fourth time and automatically fade away, beginning the tale of the numbers in her head.

The story went like this, briefly (the full long telling took half the night): The twelve was the Queen, and the fourteen, the King—the thirteen was the thing that came between them. Eleven was the child grown up who'd fled from the castle, ten was the child who stayed and died, and nine was the good son. Seven was the well-behaved daughter and eight the tomboy who had tried to kill the King one night. (The Queen had ordered her beheaded.) Six was the child still mostly a baby, and five was the daughter who should have had blonde hair but didn't . . .

Some nights her father reached the curtain before she was fully lost in the story, and she would push herself harder to disappear inside it to the only place she knew how to rest. The numbers were infinite; that was her salvation   no matter what happened, there would always be sufficient numbers. Before the numbers there had been stories, the many chaptered stories she had told herself night after night. But a story, even the longest, must end, and she would find herself some nights on the verge of panic; while her father moved heavily in the kitchen, she could not find her way to the story she needed. But the family of numbers was infinite; there was no way that the numbers would fail. She would tell herself the story of numbers, and the night would fade away, become a distant sort of story, and by morning Dagger would not remember his visits. She would repeat the tale of the numbers slowly while she stripped the soiled sheets from her bed.

III

By fifteen, Dagger's life had become so predictable she could tell what month it was by where they lived. Each year they stayed November to late April in Galisteo, then moved east to Tulsa, Oklahoma, to hook up with a carnival or tent show. Tulsa was the gathering place for all the low-rent talent; different acts showed up looking for work—some were young new talents on their way up to the big time, while others, like Dagg's father, were on their way down.

His work had gotten simpler as his drinking got worse. They did no real act anymore; they hadn't for years now. He'd bought a Wheel of Fortune and a Greyhound Race game, which both fit in a single trailer. During late spring, the summer, and most of early fall, they lived on different midways, their trailer packed close between their neighbors. These were the good times; away from the desert wind and surrounded by a crowd of people, Dagg's father seemed happier—he drank less, laughed more, and usually handed Dagger five dollars to get herself dinner each night. After the midway closed at midnight, he often played poker or pinochle with their neighbors, and he always slept alone in the front of the trailer, on the narrow single bed that doubled as a couch.

Alone in the desert were the hard times. The wind blew too fierce and often, he got lonelier and sadder, and then one night the curtain would pull back suddenly and he would stand there staring at her, his face a complex and confusing mix of desire and self-disgust.

Dagger had wanted to tell someone—sometimes she had tried to, but the world remains closed to children's language and sometimes there are stories that will not let themselves be told. She lived alone with her knowledge, making up songs that she sang only to the willows that lined the shallow Galisteo River, and which grew in burgundy, pale green, and ivory thickets along the sheltered, mud-banked shore.

And so, perhaps worn out from carrying alone her terrible knowledge, Dagger too released it, letting it drift away from her until what remained in the end was only the terrible aching sadness, which fluttered and danced through her like music—like the notes on a scale just out of ear's reach.

Dagger met Gazelle on Central Avenue in Albuquerque, just outside the entrance to the New Mexico State Fair. It was early October and the day shone clear and warm with perfect turquoise skies. Gazelle's Corvair had stalled in traffic and she was busy steering toward the fairgrounds entrance while three bulky Spanish men in cowboy hats pushed her car across three lanes of traffic and up the shallow ramp.

Fifteen-year-old Dagger watched from behind the open chain-link gate. She had five dollars in her pocket and was on her way to Central

Avenue to find something to eat. Gazelle let the silent car come to rest out of the traffic, waved toward the men now returning to their cars, and then stretched herself out of the driver's seat, all arms and skinny legs and hot pants; her face was timid, thin, and ordinary—the tattoos that bloomed across her body were not.

A macabre blue and red flower garden flowed across her chest and along one shoulder, a tiger's head roared on one thin pale arm, and a short plump Madonna graced her right thigh. Gazelle wore shiny black hot pants, which barely touched Madonna's halo, and a faded red tank top that showed most of the garden blooming across her bony chest.

Dagger pressed her face against the chain link, staring at the woman, and Gazelle noticed her, nodded, lit a long, narrow cigarette, and exhaled, pointing over to the car with a tilt of her head. "Alternator," she said shortly. "Daryl could never keep the damn car running."

When Gazelle turned sixteen, she had run off from a Girls Home in southern Wisconsin. She had worked morning chores in the kitchen there and had taken off before sunrise with a boy who drove the bakery truck. He'd let her off at an interchange just north of Chicago, and, slowly and frugally, Gazelle had hitchhiked west.

Gazelle met Daryl in Tulsa and he taught her tattooing. She stayed with him for a year in a basement apartment until she discovered that she was better with the needle than he was. She left him in May, three days short of her seventeenth birthday; she took his needle kit and patterns, his pale green Corvair, and eighty-six dollars.

For three weeks while the state fair packed in thousands, Gazelle and Dagger each worked their concessions, and then night after night closed the screen door to Gazelle's tiny ten-foot trailer and lay side by side on the bed. They would tell stories late into the night, the stories of who they were and where they came from, or else who they wished they were and what they wished the past could be.

Two nights before the close of the State Fair, the girls lay on Gazelle's narrow bed listening to the men outside the trailer laughing and arguing and telling jokes. Dagger's father's voice rumbled through the night, then faded beneath his neighbor's laughter. Gazelle sipped from a plastic tumbler filled with iced tea, wiped her mouth, and handed the cool glass to Dagger. "He messes with you, doesn't he?"

Dagger set the glass back on the nightstand and sat up. She stared out the small slat window toward the bright white security light on the top of a telephone pole farther down the park, then lit a cigarette and tried to inhale, but instead began a racking cough.

"Put it out; you smoke lousy. There was a guy who messed with me at the Girls Home. I finally just ran, you know. If I'd a stayed I'd a had to kill him."

Dagger stared out the window without answering, then reached up to the window behind them and traced her finger along the edges of the closed window's slats. "I'm not scared of him."

"Of course not."

"It's just that . . ." she faded back into silence. He had turned from a lumbering numberless monster into a sad, pathetic man who came to her bed helplessly and then in the morning could not met her eyes.

Gazelle stretched her bare arms over her head, resting them against the wall behind her. "I'm supposed to leave after the midway closes tomorrow. I'd offer you a ride, but . . . I could get in trouble, helping an underage kid run away."

Dagger nodded and rolled away from her, hugging the sagging edge of the bed. Outside the voices rose and fell away; someone turned on a radio to a Spanish language station. Gazelle leaned up on one elbow and stared over at her. "It's not that I'm scared of him. I've never been scared of nothing like that."

Dagger stared through the slat windows at the shadows of bats swooping below the security lights, feasting on insects. After a long while she felt Gazelle's cool tentative hand on her shoulder. "Tomorrow night when he's asleep I'll pull out of here with my trailer. I'll wait ten minutes by the Central Avenue Gate." Dagger nodded and turned away.

They finished the last tent show just before midnight, and Gazelle sat outside her trailer drinking iced tea and waiting for the midway to empty and quiet, and then for Dagger's father to finally drink himself into sleep. At three-fifteen in the morning she eased the old Corvair out of the trailer park and waited at the fairgrounds gate for Dagger to follow.

Dagger lay under her blankets fully dressed, listening to her father's snores through the thin cotton curtain. At three-fifteen she watched the shadows from Gazelle's headlights circle the tiny bedroom wall and held her breath, waiting to see if the sound of the car or the lights would wake him. Slowly she eased the slats from the small crank-out window and set them on the foot of the bed. She held the curtain open and stared across the length of the trailer to the misshapen bulk of her sleeping father. Perhaps she did hate him; she couldn't be sure, but she wasn't afraid anymore, she knew that. Outside she knelt by her father's car and one by one shoved the knives from their sword show into each of his old Chevy's tires. In one hand she clutched a small rucksack with two changes of clothes, the day's receipts from the Greyhound game, and the cylinder from her dad's .38.

The girls had traveled north together and found work on the Northwest and Canadian midway circuit. Two years later Gazelle slipped away while they were working the Washington State Fair in Enumclaw. Dagger went to buy new shoes one evening, and when she got back to the fairgrounds Gazelle and all their possessions were gone.

IV

People did that—took off one night—it was always in darkness —released the last strands of love and drifted out of other people's lives. And those who stayed behind got broken—remained caught inside a fragment of what had been their life. Night after night Zach called out, terrified by nightmares invading his sleep. Dagg would go to his room at the sound of his screams and sit helplessly next to him on the damp bed, wanting to stroke and soothe him as she'd done when he was still a child. But Zach moved away from her touch; he couldn't bear to be touched now, and so she would soothe and whisper, trying to mime reassuring hands with the sound of her voice.

"What happened wasn't your fault." Dagg read in a book that she should say that. The book was left for Patrice by the social worker, but Patrice had not looked at it—already she was leaving—already she was half out the door.

Zach hugged his knees through the blankets and rocked slowly back and forth. Dagg felt she should say something but didn't know what. When she reached out again to hold him, Zach rocked away slowly and told her to go now. He was ready to go back to sleep.

"It is my fault," Zach said as she stood up.

"No, Zach. I swear. I swear it isn't."

"That my mom left . . . I shouldn't have told her."

"No. It's not like that."

"You mean she dumped us."

"I mean that you can never know what another person's thinking."

"Yeah, right. Well, I don't care anyway. I don't care if she ever comes back."

Dagg worked longer hours at Seattle Center where she owned her own Greyhound Race concession. She had bought it from an old guy ten years before, and until Patrice left and her school grants dried up, Dagg paid a guy to work the night shift and weekends, and it still brought them in enough money.

On Wednesday morning a kid brought Dagg a note from the midway main office with a phone number from Harborview Detox Center. Dagg wiped down the smooth wood counter, blasted out the water hoses, and swept out the back. Even worried and trying to hurry, she took time for every part of the ritual—it was the one good thing her dad had taught her. She lowered the wooden shutter into place, then snapped the padlock shut and spun it, in exactly the way her dad had done.

Dagg picked up Zach outside the middle school just after two-forty. "I got a call about your mom, Zach."

"What is it?" Dagg tried to put an arm around his shoulders but he shrugged her off. "Just tell me, OK?"

"Your mom's at Harborview Hospital. She's not hurt. She's in the drug detox center, saying she's a heroin addict."

"But Dagg!"

"I know."

"She doesn't even—" Zach paced away from her to the sidewalk and then back again. "She doesn't even!"

Dagg opened the car door for him and closed it again once he was inside. She got into the driver's side and motioned for him to fasten his seat belt. "I know she doesn't, Zach. . . . I know it."

At Harborview they were told that Patrice was in voluntary detox and could have no visitors for at least thirty days. A young Chinese doctor in a white lab jacket asked how long Patrice had been an addict.

"She's not an addict; she just wanted out."

He looked sad and earnest, his hair cut short and sticking out from his head, his moon-white skin still soft as a child's. "Sometimes families don't know," he said. "Sometimes families are the last to know it."

Dagg looked at the man, her own age, probably, but shorter than she was, shorter than Zach. He looked like a nice boy, a well-behaved boy, but not old enough to be a real doctor. "She didn't do drugs," Dagg repeated. "She just wanted out. She wanted out and now she got out."

The doctor tapped his chart with his pencil and looked away from them and out the window. "Standard procedure in these cases is to keep the patient thirty days. They call it 'observation,' but it really will let us oversee her withdrawal."

"There won't be a withdrawal."

The doctor looked sad and scratched his ear. "I've seen her arms," he said. "Sometimes families are the last to know it."

Dagg took Zach to Delgados for pizza that night, and he ordered a pepperoni/sausage while Dagg nibbled at his discarded crusts and drank a cup of lukewarm coffee. The room was dark and heavy, with flocked wine-colored wallpaper and heavy dark wood tables. The smell of olive oil, sausage, and tomato sauce permeated the air, so that the water glasses, white china, cutlery, everything seemed permanently laced in a fine mist of pizza house grease. From their table in the front by the plate-glass window, the clatter of the kitchen rose and slid away in waves, then rose again suddenly with each opening of the dark wood swinging doors.

For everything you see there are a thousand things you don't see. Who said it first, that vision was a constant process of selection? Dagg tried to think back now, to invest each of Patrice's moves with this new meaning, to put this meaning to the delicate bob and nod of her head. Zach rested his arms on the paper-lined table and sucked the last of his Coke through a straw. His pale green eyes followed the waiter's movement around the restaurant, trailed strangers down the sidewalk outside, and looked everywhere but at Dagg.

"You're going to leave too, aren't you?" Zach said the words calmly while watching a young girl jump rope outside the window.

Dagg put down the crust she'd been eating and took his arm across the table. "Never, Zach. I'm never going to leave; I promise you that."

"People never know what they're going to do until they do it. You're not even related to me." He glanced at her now, briefly, politely, and then wiped his hands on the cloth napkin as if preparing to leave.

"No, I am, Zach. I am related. Remember the story of the Little Prince? You called me down among the pilings and gradually you tamed me. We're related now because you tamed me. You're the only family I have, Zach."

"We're not related."

"No, but I'm still family. Didn't you lead me out of the pilings and make me your family? I won't go away, Zach. I'm not leaving. I promise you that."

"What kind of mother would dump her own son?" The words burst out from him against his will, the sound of them as pain-filled as his careful face was not.

"I don't know. All I've seen is that parents fail children and nobody talks about it, then the parents get old and the children fail them back. People aren't very good, Zach. In spite of what we tried to teach you, most people will do anything to stop their own pain."

Zach stood up impatiently and pushed his chair back. "I hate you," he said. "I hate you and everybody."

V

When Josiah got home from the video store he found Dagg curled in a ball in the dark on his couch. "What's happened?" He turned on the lamp by the doorway and looked down at her.

"I'm so bad at this, so ineffectual." Dagg pulled the afghan from the back of the couch and held it bunched beneath her chin.

Josiah sighed and sat down on the edge of the couch. "What happened?"

"What happened? What does it matter? Whatever it is Zach needs right now—I don't even—I can't even imagine what he needs. And what he's got is me, making up theories in restaurants and patting his arm when he needs a new life."

"You're doing fine, Dagg."

"What he needs is so huge—the universe, and what he's got is me and this horrible self-help book!" Dagg opened the book she'd been lying on and began to read in a stilted doctor's voice:

> Sexual abuse survivors can sometimes help remember their experience through painting, drawing, or collage; if these don't work try writing with your nondominant hand.

"Don't!" Josiah took the book and tossed it on the floor.

"Why on earth would he want to remember?" Dagg sat up as Josiah pulled on her arm. "He'll run from it—I've spent my whole life running." She stared past Josiah to the open doorway. "There's an image I have . . . a memory. I've spent my whole life trying to keep it two steps away, because if I ever remembered, if I ever really directly focused, I'd die from that. You can die from your memories."

Josiah pulled the afghan off her and pulled her arm to make her sit up. "Come on. Come on, then. He'll come home. He'll be home soon."

"Why'd she go? Why'd she go, Josiah? Why are people always going! Zach didn't do anything. . . . I didn't. Why do people always leave?"

"Come here. Lie down. Get under the covers." Josiah led her into his bedroom and gently pushed her down on the bed, then crawled in beside her and covered them both up.

"Are we gonna have sex, Josiah?"

"You don't want *that,* do you?" Josiah screwed up his face so oddly Dagg feared he might cry, and she laughed, touching his face with her fingers. "Not *that,* Josiah. I figured out since Patrice left that the lesbian bed death was inside me, maybe it's been inside me all along. Only . . . it isn't lesbian. My-father's-bed-death. As if too much happened much too young and I can't want, I don't know how to want that part of things anymore. In my head I think I want my life back—Patrice—my body. But I don't feel it, really. I feel only cold and sad and numb."

"Sleep now. I'll hold you."

"I'm sorry you're sick, Jos. I'm so sorry."

"You were right, what you said. Everybody hurts and everybody's dying."

"We did laugh hard sometimes, Josiah."

"We did. We did that."

"Do you remember Tony the thug in your kitchen? He was a good boy, a very good boy, I bet."

"Oh, he was; he *was.* I remember." Josiah laughed softly. "If I had known a time would be the last carefree time, could I have paid any more attention?"

Dagg giggled and punched his arm. "I don't think so, Josiah. As I remember it, you were *very* focused."

Dagg had knocked on Josiah's door around nine one morning to ask if he would look in later on ten-year-old Zach. Josiah had opened the door wearing an orange satin dressing gown that showed his pale legs to their worst advantage. Behind him at the kitchen table, a young man of about twenty sprawled in his chair shoveling down scrambled eggs and toast and coffee.

"Company?" Dagg strained to stare past him to the man at the table. "Oh, Josiah."

"Don't say it."

The young man poured himself a glass of milk and drank it in one long deep swallow. He was muscular and dark, handsome in a Stanley

Kowalski, ripped T-shirt sort of way. Not rough trade, exactly, his face was too young and frank and honest, his desires probably too ordinary. He had wanted to get laid last night and then he met this faggot. Now he was showered, shaved, hungry, and it was almost time to go to work.

"He doesn't even like you." Dagg glanced past Josiah to the boy at the table.

"I didn't bring him here to get married."

"He'll probably go out tonight to bash faggots with the boys." Dagg and Josiah were hissing whispers while the boy kept eating and peaceably ignored them. "Any more toast, man?"

"Of course," said Josiah, sweeping back into the kitchen. "How about an omelette? You can't make an omelette without breaking—"

"Faggot's heads?" Dagg smiled and slid down into the seat across from the boy.

"An omelette would be great. You're a nice guy, Josey." This construction-worker Italian boy, with his silver medal of St. Christopher glimmering against his chest, held a vision of the universe that didn't include them. He was polite, well-behaved, and unbelieving. Nothing they said could possibly shake him. Last night did not exist for him, so of course they didn't. He was polite, ate half a loaf of bread, six eggs, and a quarter pound of bacon, and when he walked out into the morning they would both completely disappear.

"Guys like him have a position on faggots," Dagg whispered toward Josiah.

"He had several good positions last night."

"Josiah! Don't you want someone to love you?"

"No! I want to get fucked often, and I'm praying lesbian bed death isn't contagious."

"That was good, Josey. Thanks." The young man carried his plate to the sink and rinsed it. A good boy. A well-behaved boy. He thanked them both politely and disappeared out the door.

"Aren't you depressed now?" Dagg said.

"Of course I'm depressed, but four hours ago I was really humming. Detumescence—everything shrinks back to normal again. Now I clean up the kitchen, take a shower, and go rent videos for the rest of my life. When you're riding the edge of an orgasm the world *feels* meaningful."

Now Dagg sat up and pushed off the blanket. "Do you remember what you said, about the world feeling meaningful?"

Josiah shook his head. "What did I say?"

"It doesn't matter. I was just thinking. Nothing feels clear anymore; I can't find the thing that gives things meaning." Dagg straightened the blankets over Josiah and kissed him gently on the cheek. "I have to go home now anyway. In case Zach ever does come home. In case my life comes back or something."

Josiah turned on his side and rearranged the pillows. "Don't wallow in self-pity, Dagg. It's so unattractive."

VI

Arthur Shelby's defense to the police went through four phases.

1. He didn't do anything.
2. If he did do something he didn't remember.
3. And anyway he didn't hurt anyone, and
4. If it *had* happened, which it hadn't, it was Zach's fault; the child was seductive.

The case came to trial in late November. Shelby's defense attorney was smart enough not to let him take the stand, and collapsed his four tiers into one: This is the word of a colored kid raised by queers against a nice straight white blind man. *Prove it.*

It was so painful to sit in the tiny courtroom watching Zach on the stand. Dagg kept feeling the urge to run, to grab the boy and run out of that terrible, stultifying courtroom.

Zach's testimony on the stand was simple and quiet: "He wanted . . . at first he wanted me to help him with his bath. Then I noticed sometimes he would get a hard-on. I thought I must have done something wrong or bad or something. Then he took my hand and put it on him, and then he told me to . . . you know . . . do things to him."

"What things?"

Zach stared down at his hands. "Stuff . . . you know . . . suck him and stuff."

"Why did you?"

"I thought I'd done something bad. He's such a sad guy. I didn't want to be bad and make him sadder. And I felt like it was my fault, you know, my fault or something."

The boy dropped his head lower and wouldn't look at anybody. He sat quietly and wouldn't answer any more questions, until finally the judge realized he was crying. "That's enough for now," she said. But the boy looked up at her. "No. I want to finish."

The defense asked only if he was sure it was Arthur Shelby who molested him.

Zach answered that he was certain of it.

The defense attorney was a smart young guy. He didn't come out and say Zach was lying, but he began to hammer home the phrase "reasonable doubt" in such a way that it began to stand for Zach, his fag neighbor, and his two queer mothers. He seemed to think that Josiah would appear fey enough to imply the possibility of his guilt just by being. But Josiah on the stand did not feel campy. He shuffled to the front of the room with a kind of strange dignity, like a thin, discolored puppet on strings.

His examination on the stand was mostly the defense attorney's snide innuendo, but two aspects of it bear repeating: Asked if it was possible that someone else might have molested the boy, someone the boy found too close, perhaps? too scary to implicate? Josiah replied that it was not possible. He knew the boy intimately and the boy did not lie.

"Intimately?" The attorney drawled out the line.

"Yes, intimately," Josiah replied. "I am a single gay man, but Zach and Patrice and Dagg are my family. We have lived like a family for a very long time."

Dagg stared at her strange, fey neighbor. The man who made her laugh so hard so often. He looked sicker now—how had she not noticed? As if she could stop the progress of his illness if only she refused to see.

Throughout the testimony and cross-examinations, Arthur Shelby sat quietly at the defense table, his sightless gaze distracted, as if he were listening to music coming from somewhere far off, someplace only he had ever been to. He was convicted of three counts of criminal sexual contact with a minor, contributing to the delinquency of a minor, and four counts of forced sodomy. He was sentenced to five years in jail, all of them suspended.

"Josiah, you were great. You were just like the movies!" Dagg watched from the kitchen doorway as Zach pounded on Josiah's arm and danced around him through the apartment, ecstatic perhaps as much by the ordeal of the trial being over as by Shelby's conviction or sentence. Josiah looked exhausted and sick from the trial, and he wrapped himself in a blanket and sprawled across the couch. "Being sick is starting to change things for me. I'm not so afraid of people like judges."

"You're not so sick, Josiah." Zach stopped dancing and threw himself down on the couch next to him.

Josiah glanced up at Dagg and tried to sit up. The effort winded him and he lay down again, surrendering to gravity. "I am sick, Zach. Raul was right about that part. We should have told you long ago, but it never seemed the right time, and I guess I was afraid to say it."

Zach hugged Josiah's legs through the blanket. "Don't say it! Dagg! Make him not say it!"

Dagg stared down at Zach from the doorway. "People can live a long time, Zach. Even when they start to get sick."

"Shut up! You lie. You liar!"

"Zach." Josiah tried to grab his wrists but the boy shoved away from him and stepped back toward the middle of the room. "Zach, I'm sorry. I should have told you. I have a virus and they say it will kill me. . . . I've had it for a long time."

"Why didn't you say then? Why didn't you tell me?" Zach collapsed onto the end of the sofa and wrapped his arms across his chest.

"I don't know. . . . We should have. I guess we wanted to protect you somehow."

"Oh Christ, oh Christ, Josiah!" Zach began rocking himself back and forth. Then, unable to bear it, he fled into his bedroom and slammed the door.

Dagg sat down on the floor and rested her back against the middle of the sofa. "Is there anything in his life that we ever did right?"

Josiah picked up the remote control and turned on the television. "Could you believe that horrible trial? How much more can anyone take?"

VII

The next morning Dagg and Zach woke early and walked the bike path to Lake Union, where they could see across the water all the way to the downtown skyline. Zach was quiet for most of the walk, but finally at Gasworks Park he stammered out what had been on his mind: Did this thing that had happened mean that he was a queer now—was queerness something that could be contagious? After all, Dagg had been molested and she was a queer. Maybe what had happened with Shelby meant that Zach would be a queer now also.

The day was cold, overcast, and damp, the kind of late fall weather that worked insidiously through coats and clothing into bone. They stood on the heavily tarred bulkhead at the end of the park, leaning slightly into the steady wind that blew off the water. Behind them the dark rusting spires of the old gasworks heaved up against the winter sky like some strange and long abandoned postindustrial cathedral. To their right a small hill rose up to a flattened crown with a sundial made of bits of multicolored glass shards, small pebbles, sand, and river rocks.

"It doesn't mean you're gay, what happened to you. It means you got hurt; that a person you trusted hurt you. Ninety percent of people in the world are straight, Zach; you're probably going to be straight too."

Dagg tried to look earnest throughout this recitation but she wasn't sure she believed it herself. It was the book again, the same book that had promised to lead them through Zach's childhood trauma:

Young boys, especially, often exhibit confusion about sexual orientation following molestation. They should be reassured that this is normal and their sexual proclivities will sort themselves in time.

Dagg had wanted to read that out loud to Patrice, had wanted to hear Patrice's laughter—her own insistence that all our "sexual proclivities" might sort themselves in time. Only it was just Zach with her now and nothing about all this was funny.

Zach fumbled with the buttons of his jacket, closing them to the collar and then turning that up against the offshore wind. "I don't want to be gay. I want to be normal. Just normal is all." He turned and began climbing the grass slope up toward the sundial, and Dagg, at a loss now, followed.

"Zach, talk to me. Tell me something." But he turned his head down and away without speaking, continued up toward the sundial, and then walked carefully around it. A sundial in Seattle is such an act of faith—a kind of clock only useful sixty days out of a year. Now in the matte gray light of late afternoon the bronze dial told nothing; no shadow was formed.

"What do you think about? What are you thinking?" But it was as if his thoughts lacked the language to ground them, and revealed themselves only through his hands: the way he stood on the edge of the sundial staring down into the shards of broken glass and colored pebbles, the way his hands folded and unfolded, then plunged into his pockets. Below them two children flew a tiger kite out over the water while their mother pushed a third child, an infant, in a stroller. An old woman in a blue beret and yellow raincoat fed seagulls flying off the jetty. Zach seemed to relax while looking at her, as if he found some sort of resting place watching the long, slow up and down of her hand.

Dagg sat on a bench near the sundial and stared out at the kites over the water. "My mom left me when I was seven."

"And she didn't come back." Zach spoke simply, as if he knew this story.

"No. She never did." Dagg wished she'd never brought this up now—was this what she intended to comfort the boy?

"Your mom will, though. She'll come back."

"You don't know if she will or not."

Dagger put her arm around his shoulders, surprised, as always, to feel the dense square bulk of his growing body, blocky and thick beneath his winter coat. He'd turned fourteen that October. Dagg wanted to tell him it would all be fine now, that what had happened to them all was over—but she knew that it wasn't. Zach had nightmares still; night after night he woke up screaming, and when she went to his bed to reassure him there was little she could say. It was not "only a dream" what had happened to him; it was his life now. And when he pressed against her thighs and cried himself to sleep again, there were no words she could offer that spared him or changed anything. That morning she had taped a new saying to the refrigerator: *To be happy is most basic. Most fundamental.* She had wanted to imagine that the words would help something, but couldn't bear to tell him she'd found them in a cookbook.

As they walked the long way home from Gasworks, Dagg kept trying to fend off an image hovering at the edge of thought. A small memory, the merest shift of the curtain: there stands her mother. Yes. That's what she looked like: her body tiny and dense like an aerialist, her warm brown hair stiff and high on her head like a cake. When she turns her face is powdered white and painted like porcelain. Her eyebrows have been shaved and then penciled in place. "Aren't you afraid he'll follow?" the man asks who is with her. He is lean and strong with long thin hands. His face unlined and familiar.

"Not if we leave the child," she answers.

The man turns suddenly and takes up her suitcase. They walk out through the tent flap into a moonless summer night. No matter how often Dagg replays that scene, the girl behind the steamer trunk makes a noise high in her throat like a rabbit. The woman hears it and stiffens but she doesn't turn back.

Zach cried himself to sleep that night, then woke three hours later screaming from another nightmare. Dagg lay down on the bed next to him, trying to stroke and soothe him like he was still a child. "You're dreaming, Zach. It's just a dream." But Zach wasn't listening; already language had started to tire him and he retreated into a rhythm of slow, constant rocking.

"Is this how children become autistic?" The question strung itself across her brain while Zach rocked back and forth and back and forth, and his fingers tightened and released in time with the rocking. She felt she should say something but didn't know what, and when she reached out to hold him or hug him again, he rocked away carefully and said, "It's OK now. Maybe now I'll go to sleep."

He slept again in his clothes that night. The book said that was to be expected, but how did the book know? Had the writer of that book ever been here? Dagg turned again and again to the back cover to stare at the face of the woman who wrote it—a psychiatrist who specialized in childhood trauma. But Dagg knew there was only one way to specialize in childhood trauma: You say, "Yes. I remember. I slept with my clothes on." "Yes," you say, "the nightmares and terror. Yes." That's how you specialize in childhood trauma. She was leaning on this book and hating it, hating the woman on the back page as much now as she hated Arthur Shelby—maybe more.

VIII

Dagg sat in the linoleum-and-plastic waiting room of Harborview psych ward, leafing through *People* magazines and squirming and fidgeting in her orange plastic chair. She watched as other patients pushed through the blond wood swinging doors, greeting more traditional families and leading them away to the solarium or to their rooms or outside. Today was the end of Patrice's ninety-day session. She'd called and asked Dagg to come but not bring Zach yet. Now, as Dagg watched Patrice come through the doors in her sweatpants and old sweater she knew Patrice wasn't leaving the rehab today.

"You're not coming home, are you?"

"I have a drug problem."

"You don't even do drugs! Smoking pot makes you paranoid and drinking makes you sleepy. After seven years I would notice, wouldn't I? Wouldn't I notice?"

"People go into denial."

"Zach is so—so hurting and confused and angry and scared and sad and—where are you? You talk about denial. Okay, talk about it. What is it about all this that makes you go all numb and crazy?"

"Jan, my counselor, says I have what they call an addictive personality."

"Great. Great. I'll explain that to Zach."

They walked around the grounds outside the hospital, Patrice speaking her lines as if she'd been practicing for this moment for months. "This place, it's the only place I've been where I almost stop hurting. People talk to me here in a way I can follow—they give me simple lines to live with—they say things like 'easy does it,' or 'one day at a time.' I know, you want to make fun of that, it's too simple, it's too stupid for someone like you, but Dagg, it gives me something, something I can hold onto with my hands and live with."

"We need you at home, Patrice. Zach needs you."

"You don't. You don't need anybody. Long before me you had that part down."

"Do they know what happened? What happened to Zach?"

Patrice turned her head left, then right, as if stretching her neck muscles. "I didn't tell them about that part. They'd think I was a lousy mother."

"Is this a scam? I could understand if this was a scam you thought would get you something. It's like the school grants, isn't it? Is it getting you something? Are they giving you money?"

Patrice turned her head slowly back and forth. "No, I swear. It's just me now."

"What do I tell Zach?"

Patrice shrugged, placing her hands along the chain-link fence that bordered the day area. "I can't . . . I can't come back yet. I'm sorry." She turned and started back across the trim lawn, her eyes slightly out of focus, accompanying herself with a vague tuneless hum. Her hair was beginning to both fade and grow out, so that three inches of fine ash blonde hair grew from the scalp before turning suddenly into the kinkier, wilder, now-fading carrot. She walked back toward the building rubbing the inside of one elbow with the vague loose-jointed roll of a junkie. But that was new, wasn't it? Wasn't it a posture she'd picked up inside?

"I'm sorry, but you'll have to leave now." A sympathetic-looking woman took Dagg lightly by the arm, but Dagg shrugged her off, yelling after Patrice, "You're going to end up just like my mother. You're opting out of your own fucking life!"

"I know it must seem to you like we're against you somehow." The woman was dressed casually and expensively; she must be a doctor. No orderly or aide could show up in Levi's and a cashmere sweater, Patagonia Parka, and expensive-looking running shoes. Even her haircut was casual and expensive, one of those hundred-dollar perms that made you look like you just had wild sex in bed. Farrah Fuck Me Fawcett, Patrice would have once called it, before she went clean from her imaginary drug habit and began to talk like pop psychology.

"It doesn't *seem* like you're against me. You *are* against me. Telling Patrice to stay here when she needs to grow up and come home."

The doctor tossed her mane as if a wind machine was blowing somewhere off camera, then shrugged sexily, not for Dagg's benefit, but more as if she couldn't help it. "You want her to come home, of course. To come back and join her family. We're more basic than that here. We mainly want to keep her alive. A person with a heroin addiction has an average life span of five years. If Patrice can't stay clean another slip will kill her. We think she'll be better off here for another thirty-day session. This is a neutral environment, somewhere she doesn't have memories or associations."

"A place with no memories?" Dagg laughed in desperation. "There is no place on earth like that."

IX

Chinaco had been middle-aged when Dagger met him, but to the child he seemed an old man, wizened and stooped, when in fact he was merely short and sun leathered. He was an oddity, Chinaco, as much out of place in Galisteo as she was. The son of an Argentine cattle rancher and his Japanese wife, he'd been raised on a *finca,* a country estate outside Buenos Aires and had traveled north to the United

States for seminary as a young man, where he'd been nicknamed Chinaco in a bit of casual, inadvertent racism.

Having been raised in extreme wealth in a third world country, he had not found New Mexico surprising, to end up in such third world poverty inside the wealthiest country of all. He'd been destined, of course, for better things, but had through the years failed and disappointed his seniors so consistently that he was lucky, his archbishop reminded him, to still be given a parish at all.

Chinaco had seen Dagger often before they finally met, had seen her walking the dusty roads along the river and sitting outside Valencia's store in the sun. She often sat outside the church on Sunday mornings, leaning against the sun-warmed adobe of the southern wall, listening to the old women singing the recessional as they slowly left the church after mass. "Adios mi madre, adios," they sang as they filed slowly into the sunlight.

While passing the church one Sunday morning, Dagger had heard them and had fallen in love with their gentle pleading voices, with the warm adobe wall and the strange, foreign smells of incense and candle. Here, for these moments, the world didn't smell like bourbon and cigarettes, didn't feel frightening or filthy or loud.

She began to come to this place often. She would hunker down in the soft dirt, listening, and often she would stay after Mass and slip in through the heavy double doors of the church after the parishioners had filed out. Dagg would close the doors behind her against the bright white summer sun and slip down into the cool dark cavernous nave, still holding its memory of incense and flickering candles.

It was here Chinaco finally met her. Coming out of the vestry he saw her sitting small and dark in the back pew, her hands tucked under her bare thighs as if she had to sit on them to keep them out of trouble.

"Are you waiting to see me, child?" Chinaco shifted into English easily. None of the children of Spanish families would be sitting in the church in shorts and bare legs.

She looked at him for a long time, shook her head no without speaking, and then unlatched her hands from her thighs and stood up.

"I came to hear the singing. And then I came inside to sit here so the sounds would stay longer inside me."

Chinaco smiled, walked to the heavy doors at the back of the church, opened one, and stood in the entry looking out, down the street. "The smallest things can come between us and God. Sometimes even something as simple as the sunshine is too much."

"I didn't come for God. I came for the singing. I wanted to keep the song inside me."

"You're right. I apologize. I was speaking of myself, I suppose." He bowed to her slightly but elegantly, a remnant of the urbane caballero his father had once hoped for and intended.

Weeks passed before she spoke to him again, this time appearing at the gate to his garden where he'd been pulling weeds and cutting sunflowers to fill the pitchers and vases inside his house. He wore old khaki canvas work pants, too big at the waist and cinched with an old leather belt, a faded plaid snap-button shirt that he had rescued from the church lost-and-found box, and on his head, a bent-brimmed straw cowboy hat, which, pushed down over his eyes, made him look not like an Argentine-Japanese priest but like a Mexican day laborer.

"You don't look like a priest without your outfit." Dagger hung both hands on the gate and swung it slightly open and closed before her.

"A man can't be a priest always. It's too exhausting to always behave. Would you like some of these sunflowers to take home for your table? Well, come in then and help me cut them. You don't look very happy, child."

"It's hard to be happy. Are you happy?"

"Not really, mijita." Chinaco smiled, reached across the fence to gather some wild Blackfoot daisies, and then handed a bouquet of them to the child. "I don't think I've been happy for a really long time."

Dagger sat quietly then, running her hands along the fuzzy warm stalks of the daisies. "Well, if most people are sad then they talk to the priest. Who are you supposed to talk to?"

"I give confession to Archbishop Delattre. He says to take up wood carving and don't drink so much wine." The priest was quiet for a moment, then turned to the child. "I don't like wood carving."

"Ha!" she snorted, and her laughter made him smile.

"The daisies," he said, "will look good on your table."

Dagger clutched the white-and-yellow daisies to her chest. "I like it in church when they sing, *adios, mi madre, adios,* and they sing it in the saddest voices."

Chinaco smiled. "It's not much for a child to hold. Just that . . . just one sweet memory."

"I like this part too, though. Nobody hardly ever talks to me."

"You're very smart, you know. I guess that only makes it harder."

Dagg looked down at her hands. "I think people hurt the same—it doesn't matter how smart you are."

Chinaco stared down the dirt road that led through the village. Finally he turned back to look down at the child. "Dagger, will you do me a favor?"

She looked at him with suspicion. "What?"

"Just remember. Remember how we talked today. How you came and we talked and picked these beautiful sunflowers and daisies. No matter what happens in your life, no matter what is happening, a child can survive anything clinging to one precious memory. I read that in a book, Dagger. In your darkest hour, the book said, when you are tempted toward commission of some terrible sin, if you can remember one precious memory then that will be enough to save you."

"What memory?" she'd asked.

"You'll have to find it." He looked embarrassed. "I was hoping, I guess, that it might be this one."

Later they drank iced tea on the back porch, sitting at a small blue wood table holding a white stoneware pitcher of wild sunflowers. Chinaco refilled her empty glass and offered her another pecan cookie. "Dagger is an unusual name for a child."

"I'm a . . . I swallow swords, Father."

"Oh."

"Aren't you supposed to say something . . . like a forgiveness?"

Chinaco touched the purple bouquet of asters he'd set by the door. "It's no sin to swallow swords, Dagger. At least as far as I know."

"I didn't steal the swords."

"Of course not."

"They're only long knives really."

Chinaco sighed and patted her hand. "I lied when I said I didn't like carving. It's just the need to do it I find so disturbing . . . having it pre-scribed to me like aspirin."

Zach

In December freak storms buffeted the city, covering everything in sheets of black ice. Zach felt trapped in the apartment with Dagg and Josiah—hating the smell of all of them, which mixed with the smell of old carpet and yesterday's food. Josiah had a cold he couldn't get rid of, and Zach could hear him, even across the hallway, hawking and coughing in his living room. Zach sat on the floor watching the local news for weather updates, hoping that the schools would be closed and he could just go back to sleep. He wrapped himself in an orange-and-brown afghan dragged off of the couch, sipped a cup of milky coffee, and stared at the silent television, too sleepy and lazy to turn up the sound.

The Channel Five news helicopter filmed a slow-motion freeway pileup, as eighteen cars hit black ice and silently careened out of control. Cars spun and turned and skidded on invisible ice, finally coming to rest against center divides and guardrails, and often each other.

An electric Metro trolley lost control on the Counterbalance on the top of Queen Anne Hill. Sparks jumped from the connecting wand, the front wheels turned uselessly in both directions, and then the whole trolley slid sideways without power or noise. The wand sprang free from the overhead wire and pulled upward while the trolley slid down Queen Anne Avenue, veering slowly side to side, miraculously missing parked cars on both shoulders.

In the news clip the driver and passengers looked out the side windows, their hands pressed against the frost-covered glass. As the trolley neared the camera they didn't seem frightened—everyone staring out their window looked confused and slightly sad.

All day the news station played the same footage—all day the trolley slid silently out of control down an ice-packed city street, all day the same ten passengers waved their hands as if to stop it, but all day the slide ended in a crash at the bottom, the silent crumpling of trolley into Mercer Street Pub.

That evening Dagg was short-tempered, and Josiah cranky and sick and feeling sorry for himself. Zach sat before the television trying to ignore the bickering and arguments, the ubiquitous sound of Josiah's now-constant cough. Dagg heated canned chicken noodle soup and served it with saltines and a salad, and Zach and Josiah ate together in the living room, staring at the strange freak storm as it appeared on TV.

Throughout the city the streets and sidewalks had turned into sheet ice; the emergency rooms were filled to overflowing as the whole city seemed to suffer from whiplash and hip fractures, and still people tried to drive—they escaped to their cars as if their homes were unbearable. Most drove a block or two before sliding through a stop sign and into their neighbor's cars; sometimes, with more speed, they crashed through porches or into people's houses.

"The world is closed," an exhausted policeman mouthed without sound on the news that night. "Can't these people figure that out?"

Zach reached out one finger, laying it lightly along the thumb-sized policeman trying to direct traffic at the foot of Queen Anne Hill. The move was instinctive, thoughtless; Zach touched the blue-gray screen as if somehow the feel of his hands would console the tiny overworked policeman.

Patrice had turned her thirty-day stay into ninety, and then managed something called a thirty-day "Apprenticeship Course." This title was confusing to Zach—apprentice for what? An apprentice rehabilitated drug addict who never did junk? Zach visited his mother every Sunday morning, walking alone along the bike path the way another young man might walk to church. They would sit in the solarium at the hospital, a gray, cold room filled with green plants, waiting patiently, optimistically, for a glimpse of the pale low winter sun.

Some days Patrice was listless, some days nervous and distracted; each time Zach stood to leave she grabbed him and held him tightly, insisting, her lips against his cheek, that she loved him more than he could know.

Zach was fourteen; his body insisted on disengagement. He looked down at his pale thin mother, for the first time seeing her as pitiful and sad. Her hair was growing out—four inches of ash blonde formed a half circle around the edge of her head, and below that the old garish orange looked silly now and faded. She held herself against him, buttoning his jacket and adjusting his collar, as if she was preparing (which of them?) for his long walk in the snow.

Dagg no longer asked about Patrice and Zach didn't offer, yet she watched him when he came home after these visits. He watched her watching, but found in himself even less he could say. He walked miles after school day after day, listening to the Walkman he carried in one pocket. He walked ferociously, as if walking could tire him, as if physical exhaustion might grant him one full night of sleep.

Zach rarely thought of Arthur Shelby; he avoided the store on Fremont without noticing that he did. When the name wafted up in him against his will, he would bat his hand across his face as if shooing the last fat winter fly. What he could not bear to carry was the memory of his own passivity; he might have stopped the old man, he might have even killed him. In memory when the occasion repeated, Zach imagined grabbing the old man by the throat, throttling him dead like a butcher might kill a cheap meat rabbit. In memory he had managed to wipe out the wheedling need in the old man's voice, wipe out the pathos.

By Thursday the storm finally blew itself out, and the ice and snow began to melt into dirty gray slush all over the city. Zach spent the afternoon wandering around Fremont and Wallingford, walking east to the University District and crossing over the Eastlake Bridge. He stood for a long time looking down at the water, both hands shoved into the pockets of his winter coat. Zach brought no rocks to throw this time, no cigarettes, no friend to join him. He came to this place as if to say good-bye to something, and the thought occurred to him that he could end pain by simply jumping off the bridge. He imagined Dagg and Josiah finding his body—they would know then how much he was hurting; they would finally understand how unbearable his life had become.

Zach turned and walked slowly back to 40th and then west along the bike path toward home. He stood before their apartment on Dunlop, looking up at the darkened windows from the sidewalk. Inside Josiah was probably sleeping; Dagg was still at work but would be home within the hour. The boy stood in the gathering darkness, watching the lights go on in houses up and down the street. He might have stopped the old man; he had been strong enough. For a moment the steamy smell of the old man wafted up and overwhelmed him, and he turned suddenly to catch the source of it, unable to believe that a memory could be so revolting and sour.

Zach quietly climbed the stairs and opened the door to the apartment softly so that Josiah wouldn't hear him. He hung his damp, wool winter coat on a hook by the front door and walked slowly to his mother's bedroom, stopping in the open doorway and letting himself breathe in the strange and familiar mixture of smells.

Patrice had been gone since late September, yet the smell of her remained; it hung about the room and mixed with the smells of too-close apartment, wet wool clothing, and Dagg. Zach sat on the edge of their bed and stared at himself in the low dresser mirror. He'd grown taller than Dagg in the last few months; last Sunday at the rehab he'd noticed he was now taller than his mother.

He could have killed the old man; he could have stopped him. Zach listened intently to a sound drifting in through the curtained window—it sounded like a radio playing old sad music somewhere down the street. The face in the mirror was his face, but his eyes looked larger and darker, and so sad. Zach looked from the image in the mirror to his strong dark hands knotted in fists against his thighs; he opened one hand uncertainly and stared into the open palm as if there was something he might read there. Outside a car hissed too fast down the still-icy street, and Zach stood up and walked slowly to his mother's dresser.

In the top drawer he reached behind socks and underwear, feeling through the different fabrics until his fingers touched the cold blue metal of his mother's hidden gun. Zach pulled the .38 from the drawer, noticing as he did so that the trigger lock his mother kept on it had been left with the key still in place. That was like his mother somehow—the supposed protection of a trigger guard made pointless by the key inside it. Zach turned the key and felt the two parts of the guard spring open.

He sat back down on his mother's bed and held the gun before him, staring down at the snub-nosed barrel. He glanced up at himself again in the mirror, then slowly brought the pistol upward, sliding the end of the barrel to his mouth. Both hands wrapped around the cheap Brazilian wood handle, and Zach noticed that the grip was wrong, was designed to point the gun away, not toward him. He imagined Dagg, his mother—someone—finding him. They would know how impossible it had gotten for him; they would realize then how much he was hurting. Zach adjusted the grip and stared at himself in the oval mirror. He looked different to himself and older, his eyes huge and sad above the hammer of the gun.

In the kitchen a cabinet door slammed. Zach pulled the pistol from his mouth and looked at the doorway just as Josiah turned into the hallway, holding a cup of tea between his pale hands. Josiah stared at Zach through the open bedroom door, his mouth moving silently as if no words would form. Finally he turned and took two steps into the bedroom, stopping to set the hot cup on the top of the dresser.

Zach stared up at him, letting the gun now hover awkwardly about his chest. Josiah coughed once. "Well, go ahead then." He took another step toward Zach. "Stick that old man's dick in your mouth one more time."

"Don't!" Zach tried to stand and push past him, but Josiah began coughing again, and his flailing arm knocked the dresser, splashing hot tea onto the wood. Zach dropped the pistol onto the bed and took hold of Josiah's elbow, helping to steady him until the coughing stopped and he could stand upright.

Josiah wiped his mouth with a handkerchief and stared down at the boy beside him. "That's your solution?"

"I'm tired."

"Of course you're tired; you're living. Every thing alive on this earth gets tired." Josiah leaned against the dresser and stared at their reflections in the mirror beside him. "Look at me, Zach. Things do end here."

"Don't!"

Josiah smiled at the boy and gently reached out and touched his shoulder. "The Catholic Church says despair is a sin against God. It is . . . I know that. To despair is to take your life too personally; even the Catholics got that part right."

Zach sat heavily on the edge of the bed; he didn't want to look at Josiah. "I could have stopped him—Mr. Shelby." He scuffed one boot against the carpet, making changing patterns in the worn pile.

"I don't want," he said finally, "to be gay. . . . I don't want to have to sleep with guys."

"Is that it?" Josiah pushed himself upright away from the dresser. "You'd kill yourself for that? You can sleep with who you want to, Zach."

Zach stared at his closed fists, embarrassed now that he'd said it. Josiah reached down and touched his shoulder. "Don't let that bastard win, Zach. Don't let that bastard take your life!"

Patrice

The dead do not stay buried: Patrice knows this because of her dream about her brother. Because now the dead come back to her, return in her dreams and rewrite their own histories. Daniel in the dream sits up, swings his legs out of the coffin and won't stay dead again. In the dream Patrice knows that the dead will not stay dead in us; they live, they are always sitting up in coffins, changing their lives and so our memories.

In the dream Patrice wants Daniel to lie down again so he won't frighten Mother. But Daniel won't stay dead; he brushes Patrice's hand aside and climbs out of his coffin.

Patrice's mother enters the room with the now-empty coffin, and Patrice, afraid her mother will die of fright finding Daniel's body missing, lies down in the coffin to take her brother's place. Her mother enters the room and walks slowly to the coffin, where she brushes Patrice's hair back from her face. "My son . . . my son," she whispers, stroking Patrice as if she was her dead son.

In the dream Patrice is sad because her mother doesn't recognize her but sees in the casket only her son. Daniel comes out from behind the curtains, laughing. He takes Patrice's hand and helps her sit up. "A woman who loses a child has lost her only child," he says, and in the dream Patrice knows that this is true, that they have all been dead for a long time now, that when Daniel died, Patrice died with him.

When he turned twelve Daniel stopped dreaming. He stepped out of himself suddenly and toward a false and premature adulthood. Patrice would slip into his room each morning, kneel by his bed, and whisper her dreams in his ear. Daniel would lie still, eyes closed, as if the dream entering was becoming his dream, just through the willing of it, through the continual insistence of his sister's voice. At first Patrice told him only her real dreams; but then she started to make her dreams up. She told him fantasies and called them dreams; they ended the same, these made- up stories—in the end she would rescue herself and her brother.

When Daniel was thirteen Patrice went one morning as usual to wake him, but that morning when she knelt beside him, Daniel was cold and still and lifeless; he had escaped the night before without her.

"Patrice." The night nurse, a thin, blue-ebony woman, stands by her bed looking down at her. "You were crying. I heard you down the hall; you were crying in your sleep."

"The man always kills the child." Patrice sits up and hugs her knees through the blanket. She hears her own words and feels their rightness, but she has no idea what they might mean. "My brother, I dreamed about my brother Daniel. He died when he was thirteen. They said—my parents said it was an accident, but I knew better—Daniel got hurt and then he left me; he got hurt and went away." Patrice stares up at the nurse; she isn't sure what killed her brother. The coroner said Daniel's heart just stopped. She knows hearts do that.

The nurse smooths Patrice's hair off her damp forehead, and Patrice notices her perfect oval nails painted with bright fuschia polish. "You were crying," the nurse says. "I heard you all the way down the hall; you were crying in your sleep."

Patrice relaxes under the woman's soft hand against her forehead. She remembers the nurse's name is Niveen. "I don't know why he died, though—something happened to him, but I don't know it."

"You want some water? I'll get you a cup."

Patrice takes the woman's hand between hers. "You got nice nails," she says quietly. "I never had much luck with that."

Zach

"Zach! You're taller." Raul sauntered into the doughnut shop and slid onto the stool beside him, motioning for the waitress to bring coffee for him and a refill for Zach. "The regular, love." Raul smiled seductively at the waitress's tired face.

"What is the regular?" The waitress, a scrawny woman in her forties, put down a place setting and then his coffee.

Raul smiled. "You decide and I'll stay faithful."

The woman snorted like she'd heard it all now, then brought him two oversized cinnamon rolls.

"Oh, cholesterol! My favorite! How you been, Zach? You're so tall. I wouldn't have known you if you hadn't been sulking."

Zach grinned and sipped at his coffee, then added more cream and sugar to the refill. "I wondered if you were still sleeping at the Ridgemont," he said.

"I've gotten out of theater now. I'm doing something new."

"Where you staying?"

"Here and there. You know." Raul smiled and waved his hand vaguely through the air between them, as if the answer to *that* question was just too tedious. "They send that creep to jail?"

"Probation."

"Really? Christ, I don't believe it."

Raul looked tired—more worn than Zach remembered. He ate like he was ravenous and didn't offer to share the tab. Zach paid for the both of them, then walked away quickly, letting his friend lag behind to pick up the change.

They left the doughnut shop and walked toward Aurora, under the highway and toward Woodland Park. "I've been looking for my own place. It's probably time now." Raul's voice dropped off and he began to walk faster; Zach lengthened his stride to keep up. They cut across the park and down through a ravine until they came to a hole cut in the fence surrounding Woodland Park Zoo. They crawled through and climbed an embankment up to the pedestrian trail, which they followed to the gorilla exhibit. The exhibit was an acre of reconstructed jungle, kept separate from people by a deep concrete trench. Around the jungle, one-way glass allowed people to watch the apes without the apes being able to see them. The boys sat on a bench in one of the blinds, watching as a huge old silverback sat on a rock picking bugs off of his arms and back.

"What's the difference between apes and humans?" Raul was reading a sign posted on the side wall. "It says here there is only a three percent genetic difference."

Zach watched as two young gorillas sat by the edge of a small stream eating mangos and bananas, carrots and broccoli, and occasionally hitting each other with sticks. "With some people there is only a two percent difference. You're probably one of those, Raul."

Raul paced back and forth by the glass, imitating the rolling walk of the silverback gorilla. The ape inside turned away as if deliberately ignoring him and then settled again with his back to the glass. "I'll find a new place one of these days, just after I find a job or something. They should have put that creep in jail, Zach."

Zach sat with his back to the glass and the gorillas, looking across the park to a flock of flamingos strutting and pecking behind a chain-link fence. For a long time he didn't answer.

Finally Raul nudged him with the toe of his sneaker. "You okay, man?"

Zach wrapped his arms around his knees and wouldn't look up. "He made me like a girl, Raul. He made me like a girl."

The boys waited outside Shelby's store that night until the bank messenger had come, picked up the bag for night deposit, and left, and the old man had locked the front door behind him. Zach slipped quietly up to the door and tapped on the glass. "It's me, Mr. Shelby. Zach."

The old man looked confused, hopeful, and then frightened, the feelings touching down and disappearing on his face like mist or light rain. "What do you want?"

"To visit, Mr. Shelby. Let me in." Zach said the words, grinning at Raul, who buried his face in Zach's shirtsleeve to keep himself from laughing.

The old man stood for a moment with his hand high and flat against the glass of the door, as if that feeble stretch could keep them from entering. He looked as if he suspected, no, *knew* it was trouble, but then the knowledge was brushed off in the faint dim hope it was not. The boys heard the deadbolt click open and the iron safety bar above it slowly draw back. As soon as the door opened a fraction they shoved hard against it, knocking it all the way open and causing Mr. Shelby to stumble and fall back. "Who's there? Who's with you?"

"Just a friend, Mr. Shelby." Zach whispered the words in a low, threatening voice, advancing on the man, who recoiled from him and took a step backward.

"Get out. . . . Get out of here. . . . I'll call the police!"

"It's a long way to the phone, old man." Raul pushed roughly past him and jumped the back counter, yanking the phone cord out of the wall.

Zach picked up a fistful of cheap plastic water pistols and threw them onto the floor. "Still selling junk?" He threw more toy pistols on the floor before him and began stepping on them one by one until each pistol cracked into sharp bright pieces. The old man flinched again at the sound and stepped back. Zach followed slowly, drawing toys and trinkets off the counters, breaking them one by one, his rage at the frightened old man growing each time Shelby flinched, each time he backed away a little.

"Found any new boys, Mr. Shelby? Any new boys to play with?" Zach slammed his arm sideways along the counter, sweeping a shelf full of glass ashtrays and souvenir plates onto the floor. The shattering of glass caused the old man to step back suddenly. He bumped sharply into Raul's outstretched arms.

Shelby cried out and spun to face him. Raul shoved him hard toward Zach, who grabbed him by his flailing arms and spun him facedown onto the counter. Coffee mugs and cheap shot glasses scattered, crashing onto the floor.

The boys began to tear the store apart, turning over shelves and clearing counters, pulling books off the wall and throwing them one by one at the cowering old man. Raul stuffed his jacket pockets with candy bars while Zach pushed at the antique cash register, shoving it sideways off the counter until it finally crashed onto the floor. Mr. Shelby huddled in the center aisle and whimpered softly, his chest tucked to his knees, his arms wrapped above him to protect his head. Every few minutes Zach would throw another book at him and the old man would whimper and hiccup softly like a child.

"I hate you. . . . I hate you. . . . I hate you." Zach chanted the words, deliberately, throwing book after book at the cowering old man.

Raul jumped the counter again and came down the center aisle to where the old man knelt. "This will teach you to play with . . . oh fuck, look at him . . . I'm getting out, Zach." Raul stepped over the old man and bolted for the door while Shelby still crouched low and whimpered, the sound so eerie and high that Zach thought he would do anything to make him stop.

Zach turned to follow Raul but stopped again in the open doorway. He could smell the old man's fear, the whole room was filled with it, and now because he'd touched the old man, the smell was stuck to Zach. He wanted to turn and run now . . . flee this place . . . Raul . . . his memories. He wanted to get someplace alone where he could finally escape the horrible, familiar smell of the old man's terror.

At home, Zach stood under the hot shower soaping and resoaping every part of his body, letting the water pour down on him, hotter and hotter. He rested his forehead against the pale blue tiles and let the searing water pound down against the muscles of his neck and back. Then, with his head still against the wall, he turned over so that the water beat against his face, against the muscles of his chest and heart.

Lying facedown on his bed, his face buried in his pillow, he could hear his own breathing like a loud rhythmic rasp, and his heartbeat, loud also, pushing the strange thrumming of his blood through superheated veins. He felt nauseous and sick all over again, as if the overheating of the shower would now let him throw up. But he was too weak from the heat to move and lay quietly instead, breathing in the flowery smell of the just-washed bedspread and his own body smelling finally of nothing but soap.

The room was dark, lit only by the light cast by a bare bulb in the kitchen ceiling, which illuminated a long triangle through his open bedroom door. Zach could hear Dagg in her bedroom preparing to go to work that night. When she stuck her head in his doorway at eight-thirty, Zach closed his eyes lightly and breathed slowly, pretending to be fast asleep. She disappeared from the doorway, then appeared again carrying the pink flannel blanket from the foot of her bed. She covered him gently with the thick soft felt and backed out, half closing his bedroom door behind her.

Zach listened to her footsteps descending the stairs and the sound of the front door closing. He lay shivering under the soft flannel, breathing in the scent of it, the heartbreaking and familiar smell of Dagg and of his mother. He clutched the satin edges in two fists, bringing the blanket up to his face and burying his face in the folds of it until he finally started to sob. He cried long and hard, his whole body racked with it, until the sorrow was for now cried out of him, the pain that began with Mr. Shelby and always ended with his mother.

When he'd cried himself into hiccups, and the hiccups had finally worn themselves out, he rolled over on his back and stared up at the shadowy ceiling. "Madagascar against East Africa. I am attacking you with twenty-six armies." It was a child's voice that mouthed the words; he found in them a strange and weary sort of peace.

Hours later, Zach jerked awake as the overhead light in his bedroom clicked on, the bright white light almost blinding him. Josiah stood leaning on his cane in the doorway, his face fierce and hollowed, as if rage had burned there for forever and pity had almost snuffed that out.

"You awake?"

The boy sat up, rubbing his still-swollen eyes. "What time is it?"

"Midnight. Get your clothes on." Josiah looked angry, trembling angry, like he wanted to smash up the room with his stick.

"What'd I do?"

"Don't!" The cane cracked against the door frame like a shot. "Just get your clothes and get in here."

Zach grabbed his jeans and a T-shirt, then stopped to put on socks and his Doc Marten boots. He added a sweatshirt and his warmest coat; it was occurring to him that he might have to flee, he might have to run out of here sometime tonight, and he wanted to be ready. He didn't want to go coatless and barefoot.

In the living room Josiah stood with his back to the boy, gazing out the window.

"What are you looking for?"

"I'm expecting the police."

"Oh."

Josiah turned to look at him, looking so sad now, his eyes looking so old and fierce and sad. "You were not put on this earth to be a thug!" He set his cane across the edge of the coffee table and then turned back toward the window. "The police called. They'll be here shortly."

Zach nodded at the floor and sat down on the couch, patiently folding his hands in his lap. "Am I going to jail?"

"What Arthur Shelby did to you was wrong, Zach. It was a terrible thing because you were so trusting and young. He did those things to you because he could do them, because you were too young and naive to stop him. And what you did to him tonight was wrong, just like that. You did it because he was old and blind and couldn't stop you. That bastard taught you what the strong can do to the weak; tonight you showed how good you learned it."

"He hurt me." Zach turned away, ashamed to look at Josiah now. "At the trial they just let him go home free! It wasn't fair; it wasn't!"

Josiah turned and looked down at Zach. "Justice does not belong to you. Are you listening? Justice is not personal . . . it's . . . I wish for you, that you had been a man who felt some moment of compassion . . . that you had looked at that pathetic old creep and felt . . . something."

"Stop!" Zach raised his hands above his head as if Josiah was hitting him.

Josiah took the boy's wrists gently in his hands. "That bastard could hurt you, twist you up so badly because he couldn't feel . . . he

couldn't imagine your hurting. What let you terrorize that man tonight was the *same* numbness—you caught it from that bastard like a
social disease."

"He hurt me!"

"You know why I always loved you so much? You were . . . you always were the kindest kid I ever knew . . . the kid I knew could *not*
have done that."

"You think it's fair he got off? He didn't even go to jail."

"His life's a jail! Look at it. Imagine the deadness it takes to be him.
I wish he'd gone to jail, yes, but not for justice! Justice is a . . . maybe
only God can claim it."

"It's not fair."

"No, it isn't. But the real question is different. The real question is,
What kind of a man do you want to be? That man taught you in your
body what the strong can do to the weak. He took your innocence
from you. Tonight you showed how completely he stole it."

"It isn't fair."

"It isn't. But the question remains: What kind of a man do you
want to be?"

"He hurt me."

"Yes!"

"He *hurt* me!"

"Yes. Now you can learn to live with that, or you can be someone
who passes it on."

"I want my mom."

"She's out."

"She's always *out*!"

"And that's not fair either, but you're going to have to live with *that*
too."

"I want my mom."

"And if you don't get her? Are you going to beat her up someday?"

Zach bent over and clutched his stomach, his eyes focused on the
floor. "It isn't fair," he said again softly.

Josiah sat down on the couch next to the boy and pulled Zach close
to him. "None of it is ever fair."

Dagg

Dagg woke to a knock on the door sometime before seven. It was Saturday, just after New Year's Day, and for a moment she couldn't place herself in the darkened bedroom. The knocking began again, this time even louder, and she threw on a sweatshirt and a pair of jeans and walked into the living room to answer the door. Patrice leaned against the wall in the hallway, draped in a dark blue hospital blanket. Dagg rested the half-open door against her shoulder and stared at her, trying to formulate a question.

"I lost my key, I couldn't find it." Patrice waited, then, realizing Dagg wasn't going to answer, touched the door with one hand. "I walked home. . . . Dagg? I walked home and I had this terrible thought. . . . I had this terrible fear you'd moved away."

Patrice's hair had been cut short again and was bleached almost white; it flopped heavily to one side and stopped bluntly, waving over her ear like an English schoolboy's. "I'm sorry. I'm so sorry. . . . I got scared and ran away. . . . We both know I did."

Dagg held the door open but stood in the doorway, not letting Patrice pass. "What do you want?"

Patrice stroked the edge of the wool blanket, staring at an invisible spot on the rug. "I wanted to tell you . . . what you said about me running away . . . you were right about that."

"Who is it?" Zach stumbled out of his bedroom, rubbing his face with one hand. Seeing his mother in the doorway, he stopped, exhaled slowly, and then turned toward Dagg. "What does she want?"

"Zach!" Patrice took a step forward, but the boy put out one hand as if even from the dining room the motion could stop her.

"What do you want? What does she want?"

"She's your mom, honey." Dagg pushed the door open, but Patrice stayed in the hallway, waiting for her son to move.

"She's not," he said calmly. "Not anymore." He turned and walked back into his bedroom, closing the door gently behind him.

"Zach." Patrice said the word so softly that Dagg didn't think the boy could hear her.

"He hurts, Patrice. You left him."

"I know that, Dagg. I know that." Patrice wrapped the blanket tighter. "Are you going to let me in or not?"

Dagg turned away and went into the kitchen to put water on the stove for coffee. She ground the beans and dumped them into a plastic cone and paper liner. Then, while waiting for the water to boil, she stood at the tiny kitchen window looking down into the alley below. She had often imagined how it would be, the day Patrice came home again. In imagination she had welcomed her, hated her, argued with her, forgiven her. In imagination the scene was huge and meaningful—the emotions large and operatic. But now that Patrice sat calmly at the dining room table Dagg was afraid to turn and look at her. She was confused that she felt nothing so much as annoyed.

"Zach tried to kill himself, and then he trashed the old man's store. Josiah's been sick, and I'm exhausted. What is it you want, Patrice?"

"I love you, Dagg."

"Don't."

"I do . . . I love you. . . . I've been thinking about that part a lot."

"It's always a scam with you. Did they throw you out of the hospital?"

"I left. I ran off."

"You're good at that."

Patrice got up and leaned against the kitchen doorway, watching the steam rise out of the cone of coffee. "I didn't know how much you hated me. You call it love but you hate me so much."

Dagg stared at her without speaking. It was true, wasn't it? She told herself she loved Patrice, but what she felt was something old and dry in her throat, something as dusty and dead as *annoyed*. "I did love you," she said finally. The words sounded flat to her. "I don't feel anything much anymore." Dagg poured coffee into two mugs, added cream to Patrice's, and handed it to her.

"Uh . . . just black, Dagg. . . . I gave up cream at the rehab. I'm . . . well, I'm on a diet."

"Black." Dagg said quietly, taking the mug back from Patrice and pouring the coffee down the drain. "Make your own coffee." She dressed as quickly as she could and then left for work. When she left, Patrice was still seated at the dining table, staring at Zach's closed bedroom door.

For the first week the women were polite but formal with each other, as if they were strangers joined by circumstance, sharing a bench on a train. Patrice was Zach's mother, she belonged where he lived. But aside from that connection, she seemed alien and foreign now, like a vaguely annoying stranger.

During the day they spoke as they passed in the apartment, and at night they slept side by side in the bed without ever letting their bodies touch. Finally, one night Patrice reached across the darkness and tried to stroke Dagg's arm, but Dagg pulled away and settled farther toward her side of the bed. Patrice propped herself on one elbow and brushed her hair back from her face. "You don't want me. OK. Do you want me to leave?"

Dagg rolled onto her back and stared up at the ceiling. "You can stay, if that's your question. . . . I just don't feel very much."

"Stay and you'll just hate me forever. Am I supposed to be relieved by that?"

Dagg clicked the bedside lamp to its lowest setting, then sat up against the wall and stared down at her own hands. They seemed foreign to her suddenly, too thin and young and not her own. She stretched her legs under the covers and stroked the narrow mound they made in the bed. Her father had long ago hurt this body—she stared again at the shape her legs made, wanting to say the words aloud but not quite able to feel them. She had no scars, for one thing, no scars beyond the subtle marks of the collapsed chest and rounded shoulders, tucked down pelvis and frozen hips. She'd forgotten her father had done those things; she'd set those things aside in her mind just as he had. Dagg pulled the blanket to her chest. "I don't know what love is, Patrice."

"Why don't you leave? You think about leaving."

"It's winter and I have no money; I owe someone named MasterCard seven thousand dollars." Dagg propped the bed pillows behind her. "Seven thousand, can you believe it? I finally called and yelled at them. I said, 'You're lending money to a sword swallower—are you out of your minds?' That seemed to snap them out of it and they cut off my credit. I pay the minimum they say each month, which means it will take forty-three years to repay them."

"Seven thousand dollars?"

"What was I supposed to do? You were gone but Zach kept eating. He kept eating and growing and eating and growing, and so did I, for chrissake. Have you looked at his feet since you've been home? He grew boats all of a sudden—like first of all his feet grew, and then just in the last two months he finally grew to fit them."

Patrice turned on her side and stretched out against Dagg, resting her head on her partner's shoulder. "What size shoe does he wear now?"

"Something huge . . . I can't remember. . . . Is there something like a size thirty-two?"

Patrice laughed and slapped at Dagg's hip with her hand. "They're not that big!"

"I don't know then . . . size ten or eleven?"

"He's handsome, isn't he?"

Dagg smiled at her. "Yes, he's handsome—and sensitive, decent, and kind. How did he end up those things, Patrice? We're both such losers."

"We're not losers, Dagg; we're lesbians. It's a cultural thing that makes people confuse them."

"Everything cost money . . . one-fifty-eight a pound for hamburger, a hundred and thirty bucks for Zach's boots."

"A hundred and thirty dollars for boots? Why didn't you buy him something cheaper?"

"Those were cheaper. . . . The good ones were a hundred and eighty. I could have bought him those cheap yellow things they sell in bins at Safeway, but it seemed kind of cruel given everything else. A kid should like his shoes, at least."

Patrice leaned across Dagg and switched off the light. "Josiah's been talking about needing more help at the video store—someone to manage it temporarily, until he gets his—"

"It's not temporary anymore."

"I know . . . I know that." Patrice settled back onto her side of the bed and exhaled slowly. "If you want me to leave, just say so. But I want to stay. I mean that. And we can work the rest out later."

"You're his mom. You belong here."

"He won't even talk to me, Dagg!"

Dagg stretched her arms above her in the darkness. "Yeah, but he needs you to stay. So . . . I don't know about the rest."

Patrice reached out and rubbed her shoulder. "We'll work it out."

"Yeah, but . . . can I ask you something?" In the darkness she could feel Patrice stiffen. "Did you do drugs, really? Did you really do drugs and me not notice?"

"Do we need to talk about it tonight?"

"No, but—"

"I believed I was a drug addict. No . . . it's really even weirder— I was willing, I was willing to be one. I thought that if *they* believed I was a drug addict then someone could help me. There are cures for drug addiction, but what's the cure for bughouse crazy? It got too much all of a sudden: what happened to Zach; we had no money—"

"We did."

"It's a question of perspective, isn't it? There was no money—we had no money."

"I bring home fifty or sixty-five bucks every night."

"That isn't money . . . it's spare change. It buys food and pays the gas bill, but it's never going to change your life. I got so afraid—the lack of choices; the dirt in other people's carpets—nothing is so filthy as a carpet other people used for twenty years before you. And you—" Dagg stiffened, freezing her face into a neutral expression although it was pitch black in the room. "You have a way of making other people feel wrong. I spent too long feeling like you loved me but I never really measured up."

"Well, you—"

"It's like living with a nail file, Dagg. It's just a little thing, but still it wears you down in the end."

"I wanted to be safe," Dagg said.

"You wanted a mother."

Dagg turned her hand upward and gazed at her palm. "Everybody wants a mother."

"Mental illness—it's such a gentle expression. All I know is that I was riding the Wallingford bus home from downtown and I couldn't make myself get off. It was a small decision, the tiniest decision, or . . . it wasn't even a decision. It was a recognition really. I couldn't get off; something had snapped and I'd lost it. I stayed on the bus to the end of the line and then stayed on back to downtown. I sat in the back bench seat in the far left corner. I remember thinking at one point. "It's okay . . . it's okay. . . . I'll just live *here*. Here in the backseat; I've got padding on two sides of me . . . as if that would be enough that I could make a life.

"The driver gets back to the transfer station—a young black guy in his twenties—he made me think of Zach's dad—he says, 'You got to get off here, lady. End of the line now.'

"I just stared at him until he opened the door and got down. He walked back to the bus just below my window. He said, 'Come on now, take your bad day somewhere else.'

"I just kept looking at him. I thought, this man will save me. He'll see that I'm crazy and something will change. He walks over to the shift mechanic and shakes his head. 'Call Harborview,' he says, 'We got ourselves a Bughouse Crazy.'

"I nod my head at them through the window. Bughouse Crazy. Not an official diagnosis but I swear to God it fit.

"'Maybe it's drugs,' the shift mechanic says.

"Drugs, I think. That's what I need now. I checked myself into detox hoping to get medicated."

"What about the tracks?" Dagg glanced at Patrice's covered arms. "The doctor said your arms had tracks."

"Safety-pin pricks. They're not that smart, Dagg."

"Does it ever bother you to think Washington taxpayers shelled out—"

"Just listen now, OK, Dagg?" Patrice rubbed her arms through the sleeves of her nightshirt. "Going into rehab, you know . . . I was trying to rebuild something. I was trying to protect Zach. I wanted . . . I didn't want. I didn't want my son to die."

A cool breeze blew through the open bedroom window, and Patrice shivered as the air hit her skin. "When I saw how much Zach was hurting, I knew that he would die. . . . I could never bear to lose him. I had to get away. . . . I had to stop loving him. But I couldn't stop loving him. . . . You can't really, no matter how selfish and petty you are."

Dagg rolled away from her to the edge of the bed. "You don't even make sense, Patrice."

"People die, Dagg! They die and they leave you, and not everyone on earth survives that."

"Zach tried to kill himself with your gun. You left the key in the trigger guard. You made it so easy."

Patrice stared at the dresser and then down at her hands. "I screwed up, Dagg. I screwed up. I went nuts and I left you and I left my son." She turned away and curled on her side, bringing her knees up tight against her chest. "I have said I am sorry in every way I know, while you have made it your mission in life to hate me."

II

Dagg had imagined that Patrice coming home would be easier or help something. Instead, the whole top floor now seemed to live in a state of constant disaster. Zach had not spoken to his mother and would not, although Patrice would sometimes plead for him to sit down and talk. Josiah was sick with some kind of pneumonia and was only home in bed because without insurance no hospital would insist he check in. Dagg had made the mistake of trying to explain to Zach that Patrice did love him but had simply gone crazy, but the boy had exploded and now refused to speak to her too. And he'd been right, hadn't he? Patrice was thirty years old; she was his mother—it had been her only job, to stay.

It was Wednesday morning; a month had passed and still Zach would barely look at his mother. "Dagg, make him talk to me." Patrice sat at the dining table with a mug of coffee and yesterday's paper. She stared at Zach's back, his slightly hunched shoulders, and then looked away again, down at her lap. "I'm sorry, Zach. I keep saying I'm sorry."

Zach poured a bowl of cornflakes, sliced a banana over them, and added milk. "It doesn't matter." He tried to walk past her and escape to his room.

"I'm trying, damn it!"

"You're trying, you! Everything is always about you! You. You! Even this—what happened to me. How come it ended up being about you!"

"I couldn't help it—"

"This is *my* life!"

"What is it you want? What is it you want me to do?"

Zach slammed his cereal bowl down on the table. "Just stay away from me, OK? I just want you to leave me alone." He slammed the door and fled down the stairs, leaving Patrice to clean up the cornflakes and milk that had sloshed onto the counter.

Dagg filled a travel mug with coffee as she got ready to leave for work. "You just have a way with him, Patrice."

"Stop it, Dagg. Just shut up. . . . I can't believe how much he hates me."

"He's hurt. He doesn't hate you."

"He thinks I ruined his whole life."

"You took off when he needed you. He isn't going to forget it."

"I couldn't . . . I couldn't bear it, Dagg!"

"It was your one and only job—to bear it!"

That day Dagg worked both the day and evening shift at Seattle Center. Her night guy had impacted wisdom teeth and had called in high on Percodan. By five o'clock the sky had already grayed into twilight, and the garish bright lights of the midway came on, giving the usually bleak midway a festive, almost carnival air. The carousel played polkas in double time, and the spinning mirrors behind the hand-carved horses caught the flickering lights from the Hurricane ride and spun them back out over the cold and empty asphalt. A few teenagers waited to ride the spinning Hurricane, while others gathered in groups around the metal benches, smoking cigarettes and marijuana and telling one another the same old lies.

Dagg had spent the slowest part of the afternoon adjusting the small metal greyhounds on the racetrack of her water-gun greyhound game, flushing and replacing hoses and generally getting the concession cleaned up. February was too cold and dark to be much of a month for profit, but there were the hours between six and ten when kids would still pass through the fairgrounds, and sometimes they'd stop and drop some money.

Across the midway the Hurricane started up slowly, with five laughing teenagers all stuffed into one car. They spun their car rapidly one way and then the other, while the entire ride picked up speed and began to lift them up and down, as well as circling faster and faster. Between Dagg's concession and the few open rides, a thin, sickly locust tree spread its branches over a wrought-iron park bench. Beneath the tree Zach sat, staring at her, his hands jammed into his jacket pockets.

"Zach?"

He walked slowly toward her, stopping in front of the plywood counter. "This is your job? This is where you go each day?"

Dagg watched him take in the greyhound race concession, with the small Pop-a-Mole game out front. "I didn't know . . ." Zach paused and looked confused. "Why didn't you?"

"Tell you that I do this?"

"What's the big secret?"

"It's no secret, Zach. It's just not a world I wanted for you. . . . I wanted . . . I guess . . . for you to know something less . . . something different." She motioned around the shadowy midway. "It's so seedy and dark in these kinds of places."

Zach reached for the water gun closest to Dagg. "How's it work?"

She explained haltingly, not wanting to sound like she usually told it, to use with him the voice of a huckster. When she finished explaining, she turned the game on. "Go ahead . . . you can try it."

He squinted one eye closed and took aim carefully toward the target hole, then squeezed the trigger and adjusted his aim as a tight line of water hissed across the breach. The greyhound rose slowly, its pace altering with his precision, until finally it reached the finish line and a red light in the rear lit. A buzzer announced his lane the winner.

Zach laughed and rubbed his hands together, warming them from the icy touch of the gun. "Let me try again, OK?"

Two high school boys had stopped walking when the winning buzzer sounded and now plunked down seventy-five cents each and took up the two guns at the far end of the counter. "Play them, then." Dagg reset the machine. "Only, try the third gun down . . . the sight is better on that one, I think." The boys played in strict and silent concentration until track twelve rang the winner. Dagg gave the boy a prize, a tacky purple dinosaur the size of his fist, and Zach watched them wander off happily before turning back to Dagger.

"It wasn't worth seventy-five cents . . . not even what he paid to play."

"That's how it works, Zach."

"It's a rip then."

"Sort of . . . only you can look on the board ahead of time and see what you'll win. The big stuffed prizes are for when there are more players. With six or more players the prize can be worth more."

Zach turned away from the counter and stared at the Pop-a-Mole. "That yours?"

"Yeah. Try it." Dagg tossed him two quarters and watched as he began to figure out the machine. There were nine holes in the top counter where a mole's head could pop out; the object was to whack the mole with an oversized mallet as soon as it came up through a hole. The game scored points for speed; the faster you hit the mole the more points you got. Zach started slowly then began to find a rhythm. He hit faster and faster, harder and harder until Dagg worried he might break the board. When the game finally ended and rang up his score, Zach barely glanced at the scoreboard. "Give me two more quarters, will you?"

Dagg tossed him more quarters and he played again, so intent and ruthless that sweat poured from his face and he was soon out of breath. He banged each mole so hard the entire machine shook from it. Dagg was surprised to find it could take that much of a boy's frustration. He banged and whacked and banged and whacked, going through half a roll of quarters, until finally he stopped playing and stared down at the oversized mallet in his hand.

Dagg watched his face change slowly as his brain finally connected to what his body knew. She waited until he turned back to face her, then said quietly, "You have good reason to be mad, Zach."

Zach looked startled, then only sad. Finally he said, "Why was this a secret? How come you never brought me here?"

"I don't know . . . I don't remember. We thought . . . Patrice and I . . . maybe I was embarrassed or something."

"Why? It's great here."

"It's low-rent and sleazy. I wanted you to know something better than that."

Zach looked down at the mallet still in his hands. "Could I play it one more time, do you think?"

Dagg reached into the cash drawer and scooped up another handful of quarters. "People fail each other sometimes. Love is . . . limited that way."

Zach stared at her doubtfully, still holding the mallet between both hands. Dagg handed him a stack of quarters, turned back to the greyhound game, and began to close it up. "Your mom is—"

"Don't!" Zach smacked the mallet down on the plywood counter, then turned away, slamming two quarters into the slot.

Dagg drained the plastic lines of the water hoses and wiped down the outside counter. "It's not fair. I know that, but she's the mom you got."

They caught the late Westlake bus just outside Seattle Center, and as the almost-empty bus rumbled north Dagg searched to find the words that could change something. The bus bucked and rolled across Aurora Bridge, and through the window she could see fog slowly drift inland, covering the western edge of the city. Next to her she could feel Zach's thick arms and shoulders as the boy bounced along on the narrow bench seat. "Your mom loves you," she said finally.

Zach turned to stare out the window as if he didn't hear.

"People let each other down sometimes. There's no explaining it."

Zach stretched his neck back and stared up at the ceiling while he reached forward with his arms and grasped the empty seat in front of them. "Mom says you're going to leave one day." He stared up at the flat white metal ceiling. "She says one day you'll pack up your self-righteous self and just go."

"I won't leave you, Zach."

Zach turned his head to look at her. "I'm not your lover, Dagg. It's not me you'll be leaving."

Zach

The same district attorney who'd investigated Zach's case against Arthur Shelby didn't want to charge Zach and Raul with a crime, and so an informal hearing in family court was called to try to work something out for the boys. Josiah asked to speak for Zach as a sort of surrogate father, and it was clear that he was enjoying the spotlight. He shuffled carefully to the front of the room and addressed the judge who had presided over Arthur Shelby's trial three months before. "We are a family like any other family, your honor. Like any family struggling to do the right things and sometimes having a difficult time."

The judge interrupted, "Thank you, Mr. Stemp, but I believe you did this speech last time you were here. Now, if you would just promise to keep your family-like-any-other-family out of my courtroom I would be grateful."

Zach followed Patrice, Dagg, and Josiah out to the parking lot, relieved that the hearing was finally over. He watched as Raul was led away by a tall thin woman in a flowery skirt—someone sent by the Orion Center.

"You were great, Josiah." Patrice tugged at Josiah's sleeve.

"The judge has heard that speech before!" Josiah unlocked the passenger-side car door, then opened his own door and slid behind the wheel. "Those were very original lines I was doing. I imagined I was Bette Davis pleading in court to keep my baby."

Zach sat forward in the back seat and punched Josiah's shoulder. "You did seem a little walleyed, Josiah."

The court, considering all the circumstances, was generous. Raul was sent to the Orion Center, a shelter for street kids, where he was to live until he turned eighteen. Zach was required to attend the Center's Artist After School Program for the remainder of the school year.

Unlike most of the kids who passed through the Orion program, Zach was reliable, a trait that was soon noticed by Frank McKinny, the theater program's manager. McKinny took Zach on as a scenery painter, taught him the rudiments of lighting and sound, and soon promoted him to production assistant. Zach seemed happy enough with the after-school program, but he didn't talk much about it; he didn't know how to reconcile two such disparate parts of his life.

"What's it like there, Zach?" Dagg asked one morning as she drove him to school.

"It's okay." The boy was silent for a moment. "They talk like art is everything . . . like it . . . they say it heals something." They talked like that all the time to the kids—like art could change anything—heal, though you could see it wasn't true. The artists who worked there were as messed up as anybody: Meryl Danners had a coke habit and her nose ran constantly; the drama teacher was a closet queer always fighting with his wife. Frank McKinny was the best of them, but he was confusing: During a theater run he was completely professional and insisted that everyone else be also, but after a show closed, the sets were stored, and the costumes cleaned and put away, McKinny would disappear for a week or more, then show up again looking half dead on a drunk. The kids all said he disappeared back to skid row—they'd seen him shaking and sick in Pioneer Square, sitting with the other winos.

But Zach had liked Frank McKinny best from the first week of rehearsals; there wasn't anything the old guy didn't know about the stage. He was a master of lighting and sound, could make cardboard and aluminum look like a '57 Chevy or a brick wall in the youth wing of the King County Jail; he had amazing stories about each aspect of production, and (Zach liked this best) McKinny had a way of hawking in his throat and spitting whenever the word "artist" was bandied about. "Art isn't magic, Zach," he said one evening when the drama teacher was being especially hysterical. "It's just work . . . hard work . . . and no man should ever be afraid of something as simple as that."

Raul had settled easily into the Orion House and, after refusing to return to high school, was working with a tutor to take his GED exams. Zach saw him often now that both were involved in the theater program, but Raul was studying acting and for the first time had a real boyfriend, while Zach was part of the backstage crew and, although Raul was still his best friend, seeing him romantic and stuff with his boyfriend made Zach feel embarrassed and shy.

"Could have been you, Zachy." Raul laughingly tugged at his arm the night he told Zach about the new boy in his life.

Zach looked away suddenly. He felt strangely hurt and abandoned. "It couldn't have been me, Raul. I couldn't—"

Raul laughed and hit him on top of the shoulder. "I was just giving you a hard time, man."

They began rehearsals in February for a play called *Zoot Suit*. Zach stayed late one night to help finish painting backdrops, and afterward Frank McKinny had taken him to Chinatown for something to eat. Over egg rolls, fried rice, and moo shu pork, McKinny talked about his years working in theater. He'd built sets for Broadway shows, he'd done costumes in London's West End and at Stratford-upon-Avon; he'd spent two years doing lights for the Ice Capades and four years doing sound for community theater. "I had a run of bad luck then, Zach—well, a man makes his own luck, don't he?"

They cracked open their fortune cookies and read each other's fortunes: McKinny cackled at Zach's, *A romance in the wings,* and again at his own, *Your fortune awaits—grapple it.*

"Grapple it? What does that mean?" Zach asked.

"Ha! It means their fortune cookie writers are having trouble in translation!" Frank cackled again and paid the check, waving away Zach's offered five dollars with a ten in his hand. "I got it, lad. Save your money for that girl in your life."

"There's no girl." Zach looked down at the wreckage of crumbs and empty plates they'd left on the table. While Zach had shoveled five egg rolls, six moo shu pork pancakes, and a plate of fried rice into himself, McKinny kept ordering more food and offering it to Zach. "I like to see a youngster eat. . . . I'm an admirer of your digestion."

McKinny had eaten only two egg rolls and nursed a Chinese beer while Zach ate. "No girl . . . well, there will be. You're a good-looking lad, Zach. Your father, he was a black man, was he?"

Zach nodded. "I never met him though. . . . I don't think even my mom really knew him."

"No man knows his father—you're not alone in that. Only, unlike most fellows, you know you don't know him." McKinny slapped Zach on the shoulder and pushed him toward the door. "Home, then, or your mother will worry . . . there's nothing on earth like a woman for worry. . . . Have you noticed that in your life yet?" McKinny paused and glanced sideways at Zach. "Is it true what they say—you have two mothers?"

"Yeah." Zach shouldered his pack and glanced back at Frank Mc-Kinny. "I mean, one's my mom and the other's her girlfriend."

McKinny snorted and blew his nose noisily into a not-very-clean handkerchief before turning to look sideways at Zach. "No one bats an eye nowadays. In my day we didn't say those things, even when they were true. But ahhh . . . what could two women do anyway? Aren't they missing the crucial equipment?" McKinny cackled and hawked and shook Zach's shoulder, while the boy ducked his head and walked first out the door.

Dagg

I

"I'm trying to decide if I should risk it; balance the possibility she might heal something with the reality of all those germ-filled people crammed together into one room." Josiah had dressed carefully in pressed tan chinos and a blue polo shirt. A pink crewneck sweater lay draped across his back; his thin brown hair was still wet from the shower and lay parted and combed close to his scalp.

Dagg had finally agreed to drive him across town to see this Indian guru, Sri Sri Mata Amritanandamayi—or Ammachi, Blessed Mother, as her thousands of devotees called her. There had been pictures of her plastered all over Seattle for weeks now—a young round-faced Indian woman with a ruby spot on her forehead and a small diamond stud in the side of her nose. Josiah had decided he wanted to see her after Maya called that morning, saying she'd just been to see her and the woman was amazing. "She sits on this little stool and blesses and hugs everyone who comes to her. The woman is pure love, Josiah."

"A hug is good. I could use a saint's hug."

"They say she cures lepers by sucking their pus."

"Oh god . . . you didn't see her do that, did you?"

"I'm telling you what they *say* about her. . . . What I *saw* was a woman who seemed loving and kind."

"That's not possible," Dagg said when Josiah told her about it.

"Maya says the woman looks at everyone and sees God. Isn't that what the spiritual teachers always say? We have to see God in everyone."

"If people would *act* like God, I would see God. Most people act like assholes instead." Dagg downshifted Josiah's Valiant to second and turned west on Olive Way.

Josiah laughed, his arm resting in the open window; he'd been cruising pedestrians all the way across town. "Hello, sailor!" He smiled as they passed a young man with a gay-looking moustache, a Lacoste shirt, and tight jeans. "Nice buns."

Dagg turned down 15th, heading toward the Unity Church. "Can a human being be an incarnation of God, do you think? I keep thinking about the Bwagwan what's-his-name. The Oregon guru with all those Rolls Royces, or the Hare Krishnas with their shaved heads, or the Moonies in the airport starving to death on low-protein diets."

"What are you worried about?" Josiah coughed. "We're just going to see her. If it doesn't feel OK we'll leave."

"What if it's like Jonestown or something?"

"Just don't drink the Kool-Aid. . . . Oh, hello, sailor! . . . I love that little twitch in his walk."

"All sorts of people get abducted by cults, Josiah. Don't you read the *National Enquirer?*"

"Patrice and Zach can kidnap and deprogram us. Can't you see it? Patrice with her new twelve-step vocabulary, wiping out the old wiring and putting in new. *One day at a time, Josiah. Turn it over, Dagg. Just turn it over.*"

"That used to mean so many things."

Josiah laughed, letting his arm bob and weave out the window, riding a buoyant cushion of air. "What kind of program does a fake drug addict go to anyway? Neo-Narcotics Anonymous? Pseudo-Narcotics Anonymous? Nonalcoholics Anonymous?"

"She goes to Al-Anon now; she says it's not as fun as AA was. The people in it are too much like me—sort of obnoxiously long suffering."

Josiah rolled up his window and brushed one hand through his now-dry hair. "Maybe the saint cures lesbian bed death. You'll come home and fuck like bunnies."

"If I want to leave I'll give a code word. I'll say *penguin, penguin,* OK?"

"Why don't you say you want to leave?"

"In case it is a cult or something."

"You think they're going to kidnap us and feed us brown rice?"

"Low-protein diets, Josiah. . . . Better minds than yours have broken. Low-protein, twenty-four-hour brainwashing, and then you're in the airport selling overpriced carnations."

Inside the 15th Street Unity Church they heard the strange sour wail of Indian music wafting up the stairs from the basement, and, following it, found themselves in a large meeting room filled with hundreds of people sitting on multicolored Indian throw rugs spread around the floor. A hostess in white showed them where to leave their shoes and directed them to the newcomers' line—a special line for people who'd never met Ammachi. The line stretched down one side of the long hall, all the way to the front of the room, where a small dark woman in a white sari sat greeting people from a tiny, almost childlike chair. Hundreds of people waited in line, and hundreds more sat close to the woman, meditating or singing with the dozen musicians and singers performing on a small stage at her back.

Dagg and Josiah sat in line behind a pale, thin, white woman in a cheap Indian sari. She sat motionless in the lotus position, and once every ten minutes would respond to the music with a strange high-pitched wail. Behind them two aging hippies with love beads and matching paisley dashikis kept passing a sickly baby between them. The baby was thin and colicky looking, dressed only in a diaper made from a red bandanna. The baby kept squirming and fussing and rubbing her small, pink, suppurated eyes.

"Conjunctivitis. Pinkeye," the vacuous-looking mother explained happily to Dagg.

Josiah leaned over and whispered, "Highly contagious. Wouldn't you just know it?"

"We're bringing him to Mother to heal it."

Josiah turned around slowly, eyeing both parents and the whimpering baby. "Don't you think you have the wrong hospital?"

"Be cool, man," the father said. "This is, what? Like the eighth major guru we've seen."

"That must be spiritual set and game." Josiah smiled politely.

The undernourished woman in front of them turned to give him a disapproving stare. Josiah smiled sociably. The woman leaned toward him and said, "Your spiritual work is to be more respectful."

Josiah gaped at her, caught for once without a retort, but Dagg leaned against her hard and whispered, "Your spiritual work is to keep your mouth shut or die."

The woman recoiled and moved her meditation cushion forward, immediately reentering her trance. Josiah pulled Dagg back next to him. "Not very spiritual, Dagg."

"Can you believe it? *Your spiritual work is to*—like she's the spiritual hall monitor!"

The baby behind them squealed again and grabbed Josiah's hair with her fists. Josiah kindly detached from her grab and cooed and played and talked to her until her father finally pulled her back.

"My spiritual work is to die of pinkeye."

"Nobody dies of pinkeye; you just stay home from second grade."

In the front of the room, the woman in the white sari laughed as she took an almost blue-black baby from the arms of his mother and held him high above her head in the air. "Krishna!" She laughed, waving him above her. She brought him down to her lap, dipped his finger into the tiny bowl of sandalwood, and then blessed the tiny boy's kneeling parents, using his fingers to apply the paste to their foreheads.

Next, a fragile-looking gray-haired woman was helped through the crowd to Ammachi's feet. Handing her eyeglasses to the young Indian man who sat next to Ammachi, the woman came forward on her knees and bowed in supplication. Ammachi picked her up and hugged her, whispering something for a long time in her ear, then blessed her quickly and reached out for the next man in line.

Josiah and Dagg sat and kneeled and crawled forward for almost three hours before they were almost at the feet of the woman, and they sat there another twenty minutes while children and the elderly were brought in from the side. Josiah's color was fading a little, as if the hoards of people, the incense, and the slow, almost imperceptible movement forward had finally worn him down. It was hot there in the front; Ammachi was being fanned by two young girls with large paper fans, but even so everyone around her was sweating, and Amma-chi's bright white sari was stained on the right shoulder where hun-dreds of faces had rested and dirt and makeup and sweat had rubbed off.

Dagg moved forward and watched and moved forward and watched; she was waiting for the one false move from the woman that would fi-nally give the game away. But the woman in the front just seemed to love everyone; her expression flashed back and forth from wise and loving to silly and childlike. When Dagg's time finally came to meet her everything seemed blurred, as if happening too quickly; she pressed against the cotton sari, feeling the solid body, deep and cushiony; she smelled sandalwood and soap while the woman stroked her back and hugged her, whispering sounds she couldn't make out. Then the woman pushed Dagg upright and applied sandalwood paste to her forehead, and she looked into Dagg's face and smiled so kindly that Dagg found herself smiling happily back. This the woman seemed to find exceptionally funny, and she broke into laughter and hugged Dagg again. Suddenly the moment was over and Dagg found herself being led to the side, clutching carnation petals and one Her-shey's Kiss.

She watched as Josiah lay against the woman's bosom, his awkward arms and legs bent like safety pins in order to fit there. The woman held his face between her palms and looked at him seriously, then asked the young Indian man beside her a question. The young man translated to Josiah in a stilted schoolbook English: "Mother says, what is the illness?" Josiah told him, and the woman shook her head and clucked sadly, then took a special packet from beside her and smeared a soft greenish paste across Josiah's forehead and scalp. That done, she smiled at him, all traces of her sadness gone. Josiah said something, and she broke into peals of girlish laughter. She hugged him, kissed both cheeks, and chucked his chin affectionately, as if she was his loving, patient mother and he a very mischievous child.

"What did you say to her?" Dagg asked on the drive home.

Josiah laughed. "I said that if she couldn't manage to cure my sick-ness, a boyfriend would be very nice."

The next night Dagg went back alone to see the woman in the sari, but this time when she entered the hall she didn't get in line to receive a blessing. She found a place to sit where she could watch Ammachi instead. All evening she watched, waiting for a false move, inching toward the woman as other people moved away. Finally, late in the evening, she found herself sitting only eight feet from Ammachi. From this place she could watch not only Ammachi's face as she greeted each person, but also the face of each person as they crawled forward to receive their blessing.

It soon became clear that what Dagg saw of people was completely different from what the saint saw. Dagg saw a litany of weakness and need, ugly clothes and bad haircuts. She noticed a woman who looked sour and tight, who'd been complaining in line about how long the wait was; she saw a rich, empowered young man with bleached blond hair try to cut in to the front of the line. He looked like he smelled of some nasty cologne; he looked weak-chinned and whiny. Meanwhile the woman in the chair saw someone absolutely right and precious; she looked at every single person as if he or she was divine. Dagg watched for over an hour, wondering what it would be like if *she* could look at each person and see God in there. She tried squinting her eyes, she tried deep breathing, but still slips showed, stockings had runs, people looked grumpy or mean or constipated.

During the third hour, due to weariness maybe, or maybe a trance set up by the constant driving rhythms of the Indian musicians, Dagg thought an older man in Ammachi's arms did seem to glow a little; his gaunt face looked open and young and sweet as a child. And then the next man came, and one by one Dagg began to see that they were gorgeous, God-blessed beings; and Dagg felt in her heart that she loved them, she loved them. . . . She *could* love them . . . the thought entered her like an electric shock. The feeling lasted for several minutes before she was knocked out of it by a burst of sudden laughter, and, looking from the woman on her knees back to Ammachi, Dagg was stunned to find the saint pointing at her and breaking into laughing fits.

"Yes," Ammachi said in singsong English. She waved her finger toward Dagg like she was scolding her, then turned back, still laughing, to bless the woman on her lap.

Dagg stumbled out of the hall, up the stairs and out of the church away from the laughing woman and the strange foreign wail of the Indian music. She walked the length of Capital Hill, down to University Bridge, and then home, trying to make room in her mind for what had just happened. Was that a miracle—what we are taught to call a miracle? Where a stranger had read her mind or heart and perhaps even opened her heart for a moment? In the room with the dark-skinned woman pointing and laughing, Dagg had had no doubt of what she was experiencing, but already, here, walking wet streets across the ever-rainy city, the experience was changing in her, was already beginning to shift or fade away. She'd thought all her life that if she ever saw a miracle, that would give her faith in something—but this had been a miracle, hadn't it? Yet already she found in herself the desire to disbelieve. Was it a trick of light? Coincidence maybe? Maybe Ammachi had laughed at some stupid expression on Dagg's gaping face. But no—in the church at least she had believed it—the woman had given her a glimpse of a vision that was perhaps God's vision, then laughingly had drawn it back.

II

"You need anything? I'm about to start dinner." A week later Dagg poked her head into Josiah's bedroom, where he lay resting across his bed.

"It's probably the lesbian influence, but I would like someone to love me. To love me and not care if I'm wimpy and sick and not always pretty."

"You were never pretty, Josiah." Dagg nudged him to one side and collapsed next to him on the bed.

"No, not pretty, but I had . . . life. A kind of exuberant joy that made a thousand men think I was pretty. Where are they now, all those lovely boys? While I am sick again, stuck in this tacky apartment surrounded by lesbians." Josiah lay still for a moment, staring dreamily at the wall. "I am imagining Capistrano—the boys like pigeons fluttering suddenly up and away."

"Swallows."

"Not pigeons? Swallows. Ha! We were all swallows once, in the old days. Who'd think such a thing as sex could kill you?"

"Sex didn't make you sick. A virus made you sick."

Josiah laughed and took her hand. "What? Not a single moral judgment, even here alone in the room?"

Dagg adjusted one of the pillows under her head. "I should have been nicer to that boy Tony."

Josiah laughed. "When I look back on my life I see incredible plumage. All of those beautiful men and their butts and bodies."

Dagg stared out through the narrow bedroom window at the electric lines crossing a cloud-covered sky. She didn't know how to balance the tightrope between their joking and the pain of this. It seemed OK for Josiah to balance it, but mostly these days she just wanted to cry. To cry for Josiah who was certainly dying, to cry for what she'd lost with Patrice; to cry for Zach, who barely spoke to any of them, and who seemed wounded in a way he couldn't begin to know how to heal. She had tried to tell Zach that what had happened to him had happened to her also. But the boy seemed confused by that, and even more frightened. He finally managed to stutter out that it was not at all the same thing—he was a boy. Didn't she get it? Rape was something that happened to females; it was for them an almost *occupational* hazard.

Outside on the street below, a motorcycle roared past them. Dagg stared at the dust-covered light fixture in the ceiling, trying to think of something helpful to say. "I read about a guy in Vancouver. Ten years positive and still no symptoms."

"Not everybody dies, you think?" Josiah nodded. "Yet each time I get sick, I get a little sicker. There is a war in me and the virus is winning. HIV against Josiah: It's rushing through my bloodstream with two billion armies."

The outside door slammed and Zach ran up the stairs. "Josiah? Hi, Dagg. . . . I got this video from Blockbuster. . . . You didn't have it at your store. Can we watch it? Raul said to. . . . We're doing a play of it at the Center." He threw his coat across the chair and began to wheel the small TV to the foot of the bed.

"*Man of La Mancha.*" Josiah read the label taped onto the discarded plastic cover. "Oh God, Dagg. Where did we go wrong?"

"They're rewriting it," Zach said, fiddling with VCR buttons. "It takes place in the youth wing of the King County Jail."

"To dream the impossible dream . . ." Josiah began singing in his off-key baritone.

Zach reached across the bed and stopped him. "Don't make fun of this, OK?"

"Well, you've been told now," Dagg sat up. "I'm going to do a chicken stir-fry and basmati rice for dinner. Garlic, red pepper, chicken, snow peas, and cashews."

"Cashews give me gas." Josiah pulled his knees up under the covers.

"Eat on the porch." Zach hit Josiah's leg through the blankets and then sprawled next to him, his head even with Josiah's feet. "Don't feed him until we watch this movie. The room's too small to fart in."

Patrice called out a hello from the hallway and then wandered back into the tiny bedroom. "Here you are. I just got home from my meeting; all the doors were open but no one was around."

Josiah sighed theatrically. "Do you go to those things every day?"

Patrice nodded. "There are twelve steps . . . you can always climb out."

Josiah groaned, pulling the blankets over his chest. "I mark nineteen eighty-five as the cutoff year—some of us began to die and the rest all went crazy."

Patrice laughed, pushing Zach over and flopping down next to him. They lay sprawled across the king-sized bed like a family jigsaw. "It's helping me, Josiah. I had to get simple. I had to get so simple that something inside me could change."

"I know, I know, dear. Don't make fun of twelve-step programs. Don't make fun of *Man of La Mancha*. What don't *you* want me to mock, Dagg?"

"She's kind of shy about God right now," Zach said, his eyes never leaving the TV screen.

"Is it true that you're aspiring to sainthood?"

"Safety." Patrice laughed. "She's aspiring to safety."

"It's not good to be a grind, Dagg. Trying to do the right thing—to always be so incredibly earnest. You're going to give yourself ulcers, or one day flip out."

Dagg stood up and threw the empty video box she'd been holding onto the bed. "Yeah, well. The right thing at the moment seems to be dinner; you can continue discussing my foibles while I go fix us something to eat."

"Foibles? Is that a word you can say out loud?" Josiah tossed a pillow at Patrice. "Has she always been self-righteous?"

"She's been grinding her teeth ever since I met her."

"Peter O'Toole *is* good in this." Josiah turned back to the movie. "Maybe if they make a movie of my life, Peter O'Toole should play me. Do you remember *Highlights* magazine? You and Dagg remind me of Goofus and Gallant. . . . *Goofus dyes her hair bright orange. Gallant cooks dinner for the entire top floor.*"

"You should never have taken her to meet that saint, Josiah. She takes things so seriously."

"Now, in the movie of my life, who will get to play Dagg? I think it should be someone sort of stiff and repressed."

"She's talking about being celibate now."

"Don't look so pained at me, Patrice. I know this story. Men take turns fucking each other; women take turns being the reason they're *not* fucking. Zach, cover your ears, this is purely homosexual and doesn't concern you."

Zach grunted. "There she is! That's who Raul is going to play."

"The barmaid?"

"Yeah." The boy groaned and rolled onto his stomach. "The hooker redeemed by faith and true love."

Dagg called them to dinner and Patrice helped Josiah across the hall, leaving Zach to watch *Man of La Mancha* alone. Dagg set an office roller chair at the table for Josiah; it made it easier for him to get up and down. Patrice handed him a plaid stadium blanket to drape across his legs. He was almost always cold now, even on the rare warm days, even when they kept the apartment heat cranked high. Dagg knew it had been a hard week for him; his T-cell count had dropped again and yesterday he'd discovered an open sore on his left calf that seemed to be some new sort of skin-rotting disease.

"I hate plaid," he said, as Patrice rolled him to his place at the table. "It reminds me of old men in wheelchairs rolling around the porch of some VA nursing home."

"One of your cheerful moments?" Dagg passed him a plate of chicken stir-fry.

"I don't have to be cheerful. All I have to do is die." Josiah took the plate and set it down suddenly as if it were too heavy for him. "I'm scared sometimes, Dagg . . . but . . . I feel like I'm not supposed to talk about that part."

"You could live . . . another ten years even." Patrice took her own plate from Dagg and set it down carefully, not looking at either Dagg or Josiah.

"Or I could get hit by a train tomorrow."

Patrice glanced at Dagg, who looked away and down. Patrice touched Josiah's cool hand on the arm of the chair. "You have been . . . you know . . . like a father to Zach. I never thanked you—how you stayed for him and Dagg. You have been, really, like his father."

"Yeah . . . but I didn't have to *do* you in the church bus . . . I got to miss the grossest part."

Patrice slapped Josiah's arm. "You don't know what you missed, you faggot. . . . I might have changed your life forever."

Josiah laughed and picked up his chopsticks. "Let's pretend that tamari is a remarkable new T-cell builder."

Zach

The Orion Center's production of *Man of La Mancha* opened April 10th at Seattle Center. During the last hectic week of rehearsals Zach had almost lived at the theater, running last-minute errands for Frank McKinny or arguing with Raul and the drama teachers about the style of lighting or the cues for the sound. After each hectic day he'd come home just in time to fall into bed, and then he'd go to school and then to the center and again not get home until almost eleven.

On opening night Zach got to the theater hours before show time and he and Frank McKinny ran one last time through all the prompts. By six o'clock the rest of the tech people arrived and by six-thirty most of the actors. By seven the whole backstage was buzzing with people needing buttons from wardrobe or practicing lines that still caused trouble or needing help with makeup or frantic with anticipation or paralyzed with fear. Raul alone seemed beyond all of it; he sat alone on a bench behind the dressing rooms, his makeup and costume perfect, staring at the back curtain as if he was in deep meditation or some kind of trance. Zach tried to talk to him, to wish him luck and all that, but Raul barely seemed to notice him and merely smiled and nodded politely.

In the sound booth in the back balcony Frank McKinny checked and rechecked the board and ordered Zach to do this or that without even looking at him. The spots were checked and rechecked, the footlights adjusted. The entire booth hummed with a strange sort of energy, an almost blissful anticipation crosscut with fear. "You just pray now, boy." McKinny adjusted the board one last time and then stretched and sat back in his chair. "Either the gods give us a good show or things will go to hell once the curtain comes up."

By seven-thirty the audience began to arrive, and Zach watched from the upstairs sound booth as people in theater clothes swept in, talking and laughing, waving programs at each other and finally, clumsily, finding their seats. Young kids from the Orion Center handed out programs while Maya and another counselor staffed a table in the lobby explaining the Orion program and what it offered local kids.

At seven fifty-eight Patrice, Dagg, and Josiah made their strange and spectacular entrance, sweeping down the aisle to the second-row seats Zach had reserved for them, oblivious to the effect they had on what was a mostly straight and conservative crowd. Patrice had shaved her head three weeks ago and last night hennaed her half-inch of new hair, which stuck out now like red peach fuzz all over her scalp. She wore two pairs of hoop earrings, one pair tiny and worn sideways like ear cuffs, the other pair enormous, reaching almost to her shoulders. Dagg had washed her hair and tried to set it for the occasion, but the humidity had undone her, and wild dark curls sprung madly about her face in all the wrong directions. She wore—Zach could hardly believe it—some sort of long silver dress with a beaded silver sweater, opaque nylon stockings, and red high-top sneakers. Josiah was having a good day and accompanied them gallantly in a slightly rumpled summer suit, leaning hard on his newly purchased mahogany cane.

As they took their seats, Josiah pointed up to the sound booth and both women turned, shielded their eyes against the lights and, though unable to see into the dark glass, pointed and smiled and waved. Frank McKinny stopped fiddling with the wires and stared down at them. "They wouldn't be your family, would they, Zach?"

Zach blushed and looked back to the sound board. McKinny hurumphed and coughed and spit into a handkerchief. "It's a miracle, really . . . how normal you are."

At eight-ten the houselights dimmed, the orchestra struck up the overture, and an expectant hush fell over the crowd. The curtain rose on a cell block: twelve juvenile convicts laughed and shouted and whistled insults as a tall thin Cuban boy was led through the door. And so it began, this new *Man of La Mancha*—complete with low-rider Chevys instead of horses and Raul as a boy hooker instead of a barmaid. Zach watched with complete wonder as the show unfolded, unable to imagine that all the disparate parts they'd been practicing could come together in this magnificent way. The tall thin Cuban boy *became* Don Quixote, and when Raul sang their romantic duets there was no doubt the boys were in love.

When the curtain came down on the second act, McKinny snorted and pounded Zach's shoulder. "That friend of yours, Raul."

Zach nodded, still staring at the moving curtain.

"A natural actor. He's got quite a gift."

Zach felt a rush of relief inside him; he'd been so enchanted by Raul's performance that he'd feared he might have a crush on his friend. But it was not that, really—it was the magic of the play he felt.

Man of La Mancha was the Center's wildest success yet. The night ended at ten twenty-seven with a standing ovation and six curtain calls. Both the tall Cuban boy and Raul received bouquets of red roses. Everyone went back to the Orion Center and partied until two o'clock, when finally the adrenaline left them, and Patrice and Dagg insisted that Zach come home. He fell asleep on the drive home, replaying the performance again and again in his head, and Patrice had to wake him when they pulled into the driveway so he could drag himself upstairs to bed.

The next morning Zach showed up at the Center to break down sets at exactly eleven, but the doors were still locked and Frank McKinny could not be found. He didn't show up for work on Monday either, and while the counselors wouldn't talk about it, the kids at the center said the old man was off on a drinking binge again.

Dagg

Whose idea had it been to invite Susan Delonge to the house for dinner? Patrice's, probably, or at least later Dagg was hoping she could blame it on Patrice. Delonge was head of the local needle exchange. She'd been a young prostitute years before, who had moved from the streets into a rehab clinic and from there to the community college, where she'd taken her degree in substance-abuse counseling. Her AA degree, she called it, punning on the AA, which stood for both her "Friends of Bill" meetings and the actual degree she had earned. So Susan was a friend of Bill but she was not a friend of Dagg; this barely concealed animosity, which they'd both managed to avoid in their few brief meetings and phone conversations, now seemed to grow between them as the dinner progressed. Dagg hated the jargon Patrice's new friends spoke, for one thing: *he's working a program; she's not working on herself; don't talk the talk if you can't walk the walk,* and on and on ad nauseam. At each flight into cliché, Dagg seemed to flinch and then grow just a bit more obnoxious until by the end of the dinner even *she* didn't like herself.

Dagg knew Patrice's friends thought that she—Dagg—was a big part of Patrice's problem. Patrice would be more likely to remain *in recovery* if her partner worked *a program* also. This was the new role Dagg had not adjusted to yet—Patrice as victim and she herself as the problem child.

At some point during this dinner-from-hell, Susan mentioned a new support group forming: this one called POWER or POP or something, and Dagg had been unable to stop herself from making fun of the initials. (What had been funny about the initials?) Susan by this time ignored her completely, and Patrice had glared at her throughout the dessert.

Dagg knew she was on dangerous ground with all this, but the more disgusted they got with her the less she could stop it. She argued against the needle exchange, against twelve-step programs, against therapy: she would have argued against oxygen if Susan had been for it that day. God, I'm a crank, she thought in the middle of it, but she couldn't seem to stop herself, and now that Patrice was ready to kill her there was really nothing to do but go on.

Patrice's new friends often had this effect on Dagg—something about their self-righteousness would send her misbehaving, and catching herself at this she would suddenly be compelled to push it as far as it would go. She became a cartoon crank, attacking the form and language of *recovery* even though it was clearly working for Patrice. She excused herself from the table and began to wash the dishes. Patrice and Susan seemed relieved to have her out of sight. She cleaned the kitchen slowly, not wanting to return to the living room, and she managed to spread it out so long that at ten Susan stuck her head into the kitchen to thank her for dinner and say a polite but cool good night.

"What is it with you and the crank-of-the-year bullshit?" Patrice had said good-bye to her visitor and was standing in the hall just outside the kitchen. She was clearly willing to *share her feelings,* and in fact seemed eager for a fight.

That spring each of them had begun to find her own way out of the long hard winter, but their paths seemed to be pulling them farther apart. Patrice called her way *being in recovery,* while Dagg called hers a *spiritual practice.* Patrice, with her twelve-step group, seemed at least linked to a community, but Dagg felt herself more isolated and alone than ever.

At least Patrice had friends and a community; she practiced service with the needle exchange, though the thought of handing needles to twelve-year-olds still made Dagg want to cry. What did she want? To bring them home to live with them? Yes, Dagg wanted that—to bring each child home and love them—but the truth was, the glaring obvious truth was that she wasn't even loving Patrice, Josiah, or Zach very well. She felt all dried up of love, all shriveled and dead in it.

She imagined her heart had been shrink-wrapped in plastic: you could poke it and prod it, but you could not make it feel.

The phone rang—a friend for Patrice—the other sad truth was that only Patrice seemed to have friends. Dagg wondered about that sometimes and had even asked Patrice once if she thought it was odd that Dagg had so few friends beyond Josiah and the family. Patrice had been folding laundry on the dining room table. She handed Dagg the end of a sheet and stepped back to stretch it tight between them. "I think," she said slowly, as if not wanting to hurt Dagg's feelings, "that you have all the friends you can bear."

Dagg did a final wipedown of the already immaculate counter, then turned out the kitchen light and tried to walk past Patrice; she knew it was hopeless already, but she wanted to avoid a fight.

"What is it with you, Dagg? When did you become the crank of all time? I can't believe you could be that rude to my friend."

"She bores me," Dagg said.

"And what is so interesting that you think about?"

Dagg rinsed out the bathtub and placed the rubber stopper in the drain. "I don't know, Patrice. The nature of God, for one thing, or what we're doing here, or should do."

Patrice turned from the doorway in exasperation. "Who on earth knows that, Dagg? Who on earth knows that?"

II

By late April Josiah had developed a bacterial infection inside his mouth, and the continuously open sores on his legs now made walking difficult. They had long since stopped closing the doors between their apartments, and on Josiah's worst nights Patrice or Dagg slept on his couch so someone would hear him if he called out. AIDS services were just getting started in Seattle that year as hundreds of men like Josiah began to get ill and start their slow, terrible dying. Patrice arranged for the Kitchen Angels to bring two hot meals a week for the nights both she and Dagg worked until after seven.

Dagg rented out her Seattle Center concession, and they had taken over running the video store. With Zach helping on Saturdays and both women splitting the shifts during the week they had managed to trim the extra staff to four and cut store costs by thirty percent. Still, the little business that had supported Josiah so comfortably was barely enough to keep all of them going.

Josiah still came in on his good days. He held court on a stool behind the sales counter, where he could lean against the back wall, offer comments and suggestions to customers, and try to teach his new partners what they needed to know about video rentals. The store was always more crowded the days Josiah held court: old friends turned up to see him, and all the real film buffs came by for advice on odd and quirky films or to share some movie rumor or trivia story.

On Friday Josiah sat and visited from two in the afternoon until seven-thirty, and when Dagg and Zach finally drove him home he seemed especially pale and exhausted. Patrice had left soup on the stove before she went to cover the evening shift, and Dagg, Zach, and Josiah ate bowls of soup in front of the TV before he gave up on the day and limped next door to collapse into bed. His legs had been aching all week again. Mysterious sores bloomed open on his calves and at the base of one knee. Dagg helped him into the bedroom, but Josiah was too exhausted to take off his clothes and Dagg merely pulled off his shoes and socks and pulled up his covers.

Patrice closed the store and got home after eleven, waking Dagg on the couch and telling her to go to bed. It was about three o'clock in the morning when they were shocked awake by howls coming from Josiah's apartment. Patrice and Dagg dashed across the hallway with Zach following just an instant behind them.

"Oh God . . . oh God!" Josiah was rocking in his bed, his face twisted into a peculiar kind of anguish. Seeing Zach enter the bedroom, Josiah shook his head. "No, get him out of here. Zach, go! Go back to bed!"

"What is it?" Zach stopped in the doorway, looking back and forth between Josiah and his mother.

"Just go!" Josiah's voice rose into almost a shriek. "Oh God . . . make him go!"

Patrice took her son's arm and led him back out of the bedroom. "Just let us see what's going on here. I'll come back in a minute and let you know."

"Why won't he let me?"

"It's hard to be sick, Zach. Maybe he wants to——"

"No!" Josiah's voice rose into a scream. He kept making motions to grab his lower legs but would stop inches before touching them and begin to pull back.

Dagg grabbed him by the shoulders. "Patrice, call an ambulance. We've got to get him to the hospital."

"Not the hospital. . . . *No!* . . . I'll die there!" By this time Josiah was crying loudly.

"Josiah! Tell me what to do . . . what hurts you?"

"Oh God, now what do I do?"

Patrice tried to push Zach out of the apartment, but he refused to go and slipped past her to return to the bed. "Are you hurting? What should we do, Josiah?"

"Something's wrong with my legs!"

Dagg motioned for Zach to move back and then gently took Josiah's shoulder. "I don't know what to do . . . tell me. Tell us what to do."

Josiah stopped sobbing and straightened his legs under the blankets, holding the comforter above his legs by a couple of inches. "Something's happening," he whispered. "I woke up feeling . . . things . . . things crawling in my legs. They're rotting . . . my legs are rotting and white and slimy . . ." he began to cry again and through the sobs, whispered, "This is too much . . . *this* is too much!"

Patrice pulled at the comforter. "Let me see, Josiah. Dagg, hold his arms now."

Dagg swallowed, wanting to run. Something smelled under the covers, and with every shift of the blanket the smell would waft up, the smell of something overripe, the fetid, sweet smell of something rotting. They pulled back the covers and pulled off Josiah's pants, which were soaked through on the lower legs by something oozing from his wounds. In the dim light of his bedside lamp, at first they saw only the wounds themselves, but the flesh seemed alive and somehow moving. As they stared down at his bony white shins they could make out corpulent white bugs eating the flesh that had begun rotting. "Maggots." Patrice said the word so quietly Dagg almost didn't hear her.

Josiah buried his face in his hands and began to sob. "I can't . . . I can't . . . how much is anyone supposed to bear?"

Dagg was having trouble breathing. She wanted to turn and run, to find somewhere to hide and maybe throw up. Every movement they made stirred the smell stronger, and she was overwhelmed by the sweet putrescence made by rotting flesh.

Patrice yanked the covers back off the bed and began to give orders. "Josiah, sit up, lean back here. Stop crying, for Christ's sakes. . . . They're just bugs. They're maggots!"

Having someone else take charge seemed to calm him a little, and Josiah sniffed and blew his nose and pulled himself up against the pillows. Patrice leaned against the headboard of the bed. "Zach . . . look in the bathroom. We need tweezers, alcohol or something . . . maybe hydrogen peroxide. . . . Some clean towels and . . . I don't know . . . something like pads from a first-aid kit."

Zach ran into the bathroom and began looking for things under the counter. He found tweezers and alcohol in the medicine cabinet and a package of three-inch cotton pads in a box under the sink. When he returned to the bedroom Patrice and Dagg had Josiah calmed down and had managed to place a cotton blanket under both of his legs. Dagg was searching his bed table for a pocket flashlight.

"Okay now, somebody hold this." Patrice was calm and professional sounding, and Josiah, Dagg, and Zach began to calm down too. "No, wait . . . we need a bowl or something . . . go find a container."

Zach looked through Josiah's kitchen cupboards until he found a plastic bowl with a blue lid. He brought these back into the bedroom and handed them to Patrice, who set the bowl beside Josiah's stomach and motioned for Dagg to go around to the other side of the bed. "Now we take these tweezers—" she handed a pair to Dagg. "And just pick them out."

"No!" Josiah tried to push the bowl off the bed, while Dagg looked away from them both and started to gag.

"They're bugs. . . . It's not brain surgery." Patrice began slowly and carefully to pick the maggots from Josiah's oozing calf. Dagg watched the procedure for a moment and then began to help. The work was slow and horribly disgusting. Every touch to the wound dislodged more rotting smell. Josiah lay back against the headboard and stared over their bent heads toward the far window, as if he was willing himself far from this room.

Zach stood in the corner watching them, as if he was afraid to come closer and afraid to run away. Dagg glanced up at him. "You could make us some tea, Zach. You don't have to stay and watch this." But Zach shook his head and stayed, and Dagg was glad for that somehow. Wasn't that what love was, really—to stay in spite of everything—to not turn away from the stench or the horror? The women worked slowly and carefully until every bit and remnant had finally been removed. Then Patrice placed a blanket under Josiah's calf and doused the wound with alcohol.

Josiah yelped and grabbed her arm. "Enough! Enough now."

"I'm sorry. I know that hurt like a—"

Josiah exhaled, wiping the tears from his eyes. "You have *no* idea."

"But it's done." Patrice taped a clean cotton pad over the sore and began to pull up the covers.

"Not here. Don't leave me in here!" Josiah stopped her. "I'm afraid there's more of them now . . . like maybe they got into the sheets."

They helped Josiah limp to the sofa and covered him with a clean blanket. Then Patrice carried his soiled bedding down to the washing machine in the basement of the house. Josiah lay propped with pillows on the sofa and Dagg sat near him on the floor, rocking slowly back and forth, her arms wrapped around her knees. "I'm sorry, Dagg," he said finally. "I'm sorry you guys had to . . . it's so horrible."

"It's just rotting skin and maggots." Dagg reached above her and touched his arm. "I wanted life to be so neat and orderly; it turns out it's so messy instead."

Patrice and Dagg finally fell into bed just before dawn. They lay wrapped against each other, feeling their bodies twitch and tighten with the horror of the night. Every time sleep would almost descend on one or the other, they would jerk awake in terror as if sleep held the horror they were trying to escape. "Don't leave, Dagg." Patrice held her closer. "I'm afraid you're going to go away. You'll follow the saint to India and live on chickpeas and rice or something."

Dagg felt the tenseness in Patrice's body, the free-floating fear that had begun with Josiah and now ended with Dagg. She imagined giving up her life and following Ammachi to India. The thought felt peaceful and unbelievable—an escape from the weight of real loving, a fantasy of rest.

III

On Friday of the last week in April Zach's theater group was scheduled to perform *Man of La Mancha* at the Civic Center in Tacoma. The kids needed chaperones, and Zach had felt free to volunteer Dagg. They rode down to Tacoma on a borrowed Baptist church bus. Dagg stared out the window and kept to herself, trying not to mind that Frank McKinny, Zach's theater manager, kept looking at her sideways as if there was something dangerous and strange about her.

"What did you tell him about us?" Dagg whispered to Zach on the bench ahead of her.

Zach turned and grabbed her wrist. "Just shut up, OK? You didn't bring that silver dress, did you?"

Friday night the kids rehearsed in their new space while Dagg stood backstage next to Carol Stark from Tacoma Child Services. Carol had met their bus at the Civic Center, helped them find the dressing rooms, and showed them where to store the sets. When they'd been introduced Carol stared at Dagg's loud yellow blouse and oversized red vest; she stared at Dagg's red high-top sneakers; she looked at Dagg's wild uncombed hair, and Dagg smiled then, her most charming smile—the woman looked almost prim and like she might vote Republican, but Dagg's gaydar detector sounded loud in her ears.

She introduced herself and Zach to Carol, and as Raul was walking by she grabbed his arm and introduced him as well. Dagg watched as Raul's gaydar went off also; he smiled a slow mocking smile toward Carol and asked if her husband also worked here. Carol stammered and managed to evade the question, leading them back to the sound board where Frank McKinny was making himself right at home. Raul introduced them, stressing to McKinny that the woman was single. McKinny went valiantly to gallant and began to flirt with her in a sort of nineteenth- century courtly way.

By five o'clock the kids were all checked into their rooms at the Y, and the drama teachers and McKinny herded them to the Old Spaghetti Factory for dinner. They had reserved a table for thirty, and the restaurant agreed to feed them for five dollars a head. McKinny had invited Carol Stark to join them, and she sat quietly next to him while Raul and Martin, the tall thin Cuban boy who played Don Quixote, argued over her head with McKinny about the lighting for their favorite scene.

Dagg sat farther down the table between two of the only six girls on the tour. They were both former child hookers and currently lovers, but one was disappointed in their sex life and they made the mistake of thinking Dagg, being older and with a long-term partner, would somehow be able to say something wise. As they talked and argued and even sobbed a little, Dagg tried to think of wise things and then say them to these kids as if she was sure those things were true. Meanwhile, at the end of the table Carol Stark kept glancing toward her as if she secretly wished she were sitting down there.

"The Republican babe wants you." Lisa, the younger of the two, with the pierced eyebrow, motioned toward Dagg with a fork heaped with spaghetti. Janet, the elder, taller girl, made siren noises like her gaydar alarm had suddenly gone off. "She doesn't register much on the babe-o-meter. Too meek and well-behaved for my taste." Both girls snorted with laughter while Frank McKinny, noticing their attention to his dinner guest, glared fiercely at the three of them and moved his chair an inch closer to Carol. This caused Lisa and Janet to begin to snort. They were laughing so hard now, and Dagg, feeling pity for the woman, tried to change the subject and break their attention.

"Who does register on your babe-o-meter?"

Both girls snapped instantly to attention and began to scan the room. "The woman in the black dress, with the dork who's probably her brother . . . the hostess in the green skirt, though she probably looks better when she's not dressed in work clothes . . ." The girls rated and commented and cruised the whole restaurant while Dagg relaxed and continued to watch Carol Stark. She was not beautiful—she was too well-behaved and prim for that, her face too closed and carefully guarded.

"She wants you, Dagg." Lisa tugged at the edge of her sweater.

"Why not?" Janet said. "Dagg amps the babe-o-meter. She looks sort of wild and animal, and she's got a gorgeous smile." Dagg smiled at her and felt how much she liked to hear that. She'd felt so old, musty, and domesticated—it was nice to have two teenagers think she was a babe.

"You and Patrice together *way* amp the babe-o-meter." Lisa nodded in agreement. "It's something about two gorgeous women being faithful to each other. I think it's the hottest thing there could be."

"Faithful." Dagg said the word softly. She had been faithful to Patrice, it seemed to her now, because their lives had been such wrecks and there had been no time to bail out. And Patrice . . . perhaps she had been faithful also. Who really knew another's heart?

"It's so hot!" Janet nodded eagerly in a kind of bumptious teenaged way. "Two gorgeous women wanting only each other . . ." It was clear to Dagg that they were finished discussing her and were imagining themselves now. She let them talk on, barely listening to most of it and glancing down the table to Carol, who seemed to feel Dagg's eyes on her and would glance up to meet Dagg's stare and then blush. The blush was sweet; it was nice to feel powerful—to feel that she controlled the way this woman felt tonight.

The curtain rose at eight to an almost-full house, and while the kids strutted and sang and moved about the stage, Dagg watched from the wings, standing much too close to Carol—close enough to smell her. Patrice had always insisted that sex was 80 percent smell; Carol smelled bland and musty, a little like old cigarettes and a little like a government office. But what Dagg found so appealing was not her own desire—she'd had more than enough of her own wanting—it was the feel of this woman wanting *her* tonight; this woman breathed *her* in as something strange and wild and desired.

Dagg stood close behind Carol, letting her breath exhale against the back of the other woman's neck. She felt no strong desire for this woman, but she wanted so much to be wanted—to feel someone else grow short-breathed and feverish, to feel someone else's desire. Dagg took a step closer until her lips were inches from the woman's neck. "Let's go somewhere," she whispered. "Come on now."

Carol nodded without speaking and turned toward the back door. Dagg had the feeling Carol was trying to ignore her own decision; she wanted to sleepwalk them both into bed.

Dagg left a note with the stage crew for Zach and Frank McKinny, telling them she would meet them back at the Y. She imagined McKinny reading it, having watched her and Carol walk out. When he was angry his false teeth slipped a little; she imagined McKinny's lips stretching to cover his angry, slipping gums.

They went to a small, dark bar and restaurant just off the park. Dagg ordered draft beer, then changed that to margaritas; it would take more than beer to get them from this bar to bed.

Carol spoke haltingly of her work and her life, and then asked guarded questions about the Orion Center, the kids, and the theater. Dagg answered without thinking; the questions didn't matter. She thought maybe it was this woman's closed-down shyness that made her want to lay hands on her, to watch this woman come alive in her hands. Dagg imagined resting her hand along Carol's neck, feeling the woman fight against that touch and then relax and then surrender. This woman wanted her, but she was still strangely at odds with that wanting—as if she wanted so much for Dagg to touch her, but Dagg was the only one of them who knew it.

Carol was not beautiful—not like Patrice for instance; she was shy and awkward in her body; she seemed to wear her own face like a strange Chinese mask. They ordered another round of margaritas, and Dagg watched as Carol's face began to soften under the effects of the drinks. She smiled at Dagg, and even laughed once, yet her hand trembled as she reached out for her glass. Dagg stretched her hand across the table and touched that trembling hand. Carol seemed startled by the action, but she did not pull away. The woman wanted her—Dagg knew that—and she felt in herself some power from that knowing. It was not desire that Dagg kept feeling, but a wanting to lay hands upon power—to take back something for herself she had long ago lost.

They drove in silence down Ruston, past the paper mills and toward a rundown neighborhood on the east side of the city. Dagg stared out of the passenger window watching the flicker of street lamps make halos in the night as rain hissed off phosphorus and sprinkled the glowing city streets. The car turned left on Yakima Avenue and then left again on Carr Street; they stopped in the driveway of a small bungalow. As they entered the house, Dagg glanced around the living room, a strange mix of tasteless furniture, a few antiques. The walls were covered in kitschy pictures—photographs of puppies and teddy-bear art. Carol looked confused and uncertain. "I could make you coffee or something." She said the words tentatively, as if waiting for Dagg to tell her now what to do.

Dagg caught her hand in mid-gesture and stopped her. "Show me where you sleep—your bedroom." From the living room she could see a small bedroom in the back of the house.

"Wait . . ." Carol's hand caught at her shirt front. "What are you . . . this is going too fast for me."

"You want me."

"But . . ."

Dagg led her into the bedroom and onto the bed. Carol curled against her arm like a terrified child. "I like it, that you want me. All you have to do is want me."

"But . . ."

"This is what you wanted to happen, isn't it?"

Carol seemed to shudder slightly, and Dagg propped herself up on one elbow to see better, surprised by the discomfort and terror struggling in the woman's face. She looked not pleased but victimized by desire, as if she wanted this against her own will. Dagg smelled lime and tequila on Carol's breath and wished herself a little drunker. She wished she felt less self-disgust for what she was about to do. "You want me."

Carol nodded. Dagg grabbed her arms. "Say it!"

Carol's eyes widened; perhaps she was afraid now. Dagg grabbed her harder. "Tell me what you want from me."

"I . . ." Carol tried to reach up to bring Dagg's mouth down to her; she seemed desperate for a way to make Dagg shut up, but Dagg kept just out of reach of her. "You want me . . . I want to hear you say it."

"No . . . I . . . don't. . . . I want . . ."

"Don't lie . . . you want it, but you want to pretend things are sweet, like your teddy-bear art. You don't want sweet, I know that. What you really want is to get laid."

"Don't!"

"Hard, right? You want me to fuck you till your brains come out." Dagg slid down next to her and held her tightly. "I will . . . I will just as soon as you say it."

Carol shivered against her body, and Dagg noticed for the first time how cold it was inside the house. She pulled the blankets up and covered them both. Carol's arms made a fortress between them, and though the sheets were starting to warm, her shivering didn't stop. Dagg reached for her blouse and began unbuttoning it, but Carol stopped her, grasping her wrist with an icy hand. "Why are you doing this? You act like you hate me."

"I hate lies, mostly. . . . I hate people who feel things and pretend that they don't."

Carol sat up suddenly, shoving Dagg off her with surprising strength. "You don't know me. You don't . . ."

"Yeah . . . I do. . . . I know how you are." Dagg rolled onto her back, watching Carol's face seem to twist between rage and desire. Maybe rage would win. She would jump from the bed and throw Dagg out the door. Maybe desire would win and she would swallow pride and beg for touching. Dagg felt surprised by how little any of it mattered; she crossed her arms behind her head and felt the heavy metal bracelet Ammachi had given her clank against the wooden headboard. The sound was funny; the scene was—this newly converted spiritual seeker wanting to make a woman she didn't care for beg. *I'm a little confused,* she told herself silently. Just saying it to herself made her want to start to laugh. She wanted to tell Patrice this story, or maybe Josiah. She wanted to tell all of it, complete with the Ammachi bracelet banging on wood. Carol uncurled from herself and lay back now. "I want you," she said quietly. "I want you."

Dagg could hardly say no then, could she? She could hardly beg off and explain about Patrice, Josiah's laughter, and the Ammachi bracelet clanking against wood. So she made love to the woman using all the skill and rage and sorrow she had. And when they had finished, and the sorrow and rage had finally poured out, Dagg felt tender toward her, toward all of them, really. Human beings were odd and dear, pathetic creatures.

Dagg kissed Carol's forehead and covered them both with the tangled blankets. Carol murmured something and Dagg shushed her again and smoothed back her hair. She fell asleep, finally, while staring at the shadows the streetlight formed across one wall. She had been unfaithful to Patrice tonight; she had made love to a woman whose smell she didn't even care for, and yet now, with the stranger wrapped tightly against her and the shadows of traffic circling the walls, she felt no shame in herself and no betrayal. How odd to find that what Dagg felt for both women was an overwhelming tenderness and something perhaps close to love.

Dagg woke the next morning before sunrise, slipped out of bed, and dressed hurriedly in the cold living room. She walked back down to Ruston and caught a bus toward town, staring out the rain-splattered windows and hoping to spot a coffee shop or café. As the bus rumbled into downtown Tacoma, Dagg lifted one hand to her face and breathed in the pungent smell of the stranger. She didn't know what she would tell Patrice; she didn't know what she would say. The smell on her hands was the power she had wanted; it didn't seem to mean much now.

Zach

They broke down sets in Tacoma after the last Sunday show, and on the bus back to Seattle McKinny sat next to Zach. The weekend shows had been tremendous successes, and Zach felt both exhilarated and exhausted at once. "Good work on the boards, Zach." McKinny patted the boy's shoulder.

Zach turned away, stretching one long leg into the front aisle of the bus. "Are you going to disappear tomorrow?"

"Is that what's on your mind?"

"Maybe it's true. You are a drunk."

McKinny laughed shortly and slapped the seat back. "Are you going to spend your whole life thinking other people are letting you down?"

"They do, don't they?"

"Nobody's perfect, son. Coming from your family, one would think you would have noticed that." McKinny settled back into the seat and seemed to forget Zach was there for the rest of the ride.

That night Zach knocked on Raul's door after the halls had been cleared and the counselors made bed check. "What are you doing?" Raul whispered, half opening the door. Behind him in the darkness by the open window, Zach could see the bright red glow of someone's cigarette.

"Nothing, Raul. I wasn't sleepy."

Raul lounged in the open doorway, dressed only in a pair of red silk boxer shorts. His body was wiry and thin and liquid. One hand rubbed at his smooth, hairless chest. Behind him a chair shifted in the darkness; Zach could see Martin's long silhouette. "McKinny drinks too much. Did you know that?"

Raul laughed and took another step into the hallway, gently closing the door behind him. "I have company. What's on your mind, Zach?"

Zach watched him scratch his thigh through the thin shorts. "Are you . . .?" He stopped, unable to imagine the words he needed. Raul seemed so strange to him now, so foreign. In a moment Raul would go back into his room; Zach tried to imagine the things he and Martin did there. "Do you kiss him? On the lips, I mean. Like a girl?"

Raul smiled lazily at the taller boy, looked up and down the hall, then tilted his head up and kissed Zach's lips gently. The boy pulled back, startled, then stepped backward. "I don't want—"

Raul laughed. "You're such a kid, Zach. But it means something different now, to want to sleep over."

Zach tossed and turned and couldn't sleep that night. He kept feeling Raul's lips on his own like a burn. He would tell himself to forget it, to just go to sleep now, but as sleep began to envelop him he would feel the velvet softness of the older boy's lips and would wipe at his face roughly as if trying to remove even the memory. In the morning he sat upright in bed, resting his lips softly again and again on the back of his own hand. Raul's lips had felt like that last night.

Dagg

On Monday, a week after Dagg and Zach got home from Tacoma, Josiah spiked a fever of one hundred seven. Patrice called for an ambulance while Zach and Dagg struggled to wrestle him into a bathtub filled with icy water, and by the time the paramedics arrived he was soaked and cold but somewhat back in his senses. "Don't send me to the hospital."

"You're bad off, Josiah . . . you have to go."

"I'll die there . . . people always die there!"

One of the medics was gay and that helped a little. He wasn't afraid of Josiah, for one thing. He talked and coaxed him into dry clothes, then half carried him in his arms down the stairs when Josiah refused to lie down on their litter.

Patrice dealt with the hospital paperwork while Dagg and Zach followed Josiah's wheelchair to his room. "Don't let them put me in a hospital gown . . . it will be too much to look that pathetic!" Josiah fought off a young nurse's aid, who tried to offer him a hospital gown. Zach offered to fetch Josiah some pajamas and fled the room, looking grateful for a reason to escape back to the house. Dagg pulled a plastic chair close to the bed and sank into it, resting her feet on the metal bed rail. Two nurses and a lab tech bustled in together, moved her out of their way, and began to hook Josiah to lines of saline and antibiotics strung above his bed.

He was dying: Dagg suddenly knew that, and everything that was happening was only meant to delay that as long as they could. She stared over the strangers' backs to Josiah; his face was suddenly foreign to her. He slept most of the afternoon and evening; they brought a supper tray but he didn't touch it. His breathing was deep and regular, so that even with his eyes open he sounded fast asleep.

144

Dagg stayed until dusk, then went home to eat dinner. They all came back again for visiting hours and lay on the other empty bed in the room, watching TV with the sound turned low. The Sonics were playing the Suns in Phoenix, but even Zach didn't care about the basketball game. Still, the TV gave them something to look at; it was terrible to look at Josiah, and hardly much better to look at one another. He looked *old* so suddenly, as if his face which had been shriveling slowly, had suddenly caved in today. One arm lay awkwardly under the sheet while the other was tied to his bed rail, stuck with first aid tape and tubes and needles.

Sometimes he'd wake and look around him and make some lame joke, but mostly he just slept or half-slept while Patrice, Dagg, and Zach stared at the silent TV or walked in the halls or talked quietly with each other. At nine, the end of visiting hours, Patrice and Dagg agreed that Patrice and Zach should go home, but Zach didn't want to leave Josiah and began to argue with his mother. In the midst of it, Josiah sat up. "I am dying here," he said quietly. "Try to keep things down a little." Zach burst into tears and threw himself across the foot of Josiah's hospital bed, and Josiah stroked Zach's head softly and hushed him. "Don't be afraid. You don't have to be afraid now."

Josiah had entered a state of semiconsciousness where he seemed to them alternately out of his mind or quite wise. The nurse said he wasn't getting enough oxygen—something about swelling and fluid in his lungs. She said it was important for family to keep him oriented, but it seemed to Dagg that, given his true circumstances, the other world he drifted to seemed a better place to rest.

Patrice led Zach out of the room after kissing both Dagg and Josiah good night, and Dagg settled into the empty spare bed and watched the end of the Sonics game while listening to Josiah's uneven breathing. By ten all visitors had left the hospital, lights were dimmed in the hallways, and the floor settled into the strange and bizarre life of a hospital at night. A nurse woke Josiah at twelve to offer him a sleeping pill; he took it, mumbling something about his mother. By one the place was almost silent except for footsteps in the hallways and, somewhere far down the corridor, the thin, high-pitched wail of a very young child.

The room was shadowy and strange, lit partly by orange dials on the bedside machines and partly by the hall lights glowing through the open doorway. Dagg had tried closing the door, but orderlies and night nurses kept entering to check on things and leaving it open whenever they went out. She felt annoyed at first, but then it occurred to her that they too wanted to protect Josiah—only because they were hospital people and they thought perhaps it was Dagg, the outsider, he would need protection from.

The night was long, longer than any other in her memory, or at least any other since she'd been a child. It had that feel to it—a long night of silent fearfulness—only now Dagg felt as if she was keeping watch for Josiah. Something was sneaking up on him—something shadowy and terrifying, something awful and familiar. Perhaps if she kept watch beside him, Dagg could keep that thing from coming—it felt sometimes like a visitor to her, who would arrive from somewhere else, and sometimes like a thing that lurked inside Josiah, waiting patiently to bloom.

Sometimes Josiah would sit up suddenly, calling out some stranger's name.

"What do you need, Josiah?" Dagg would sit up also and they would stare at each other across the gulf of shadowy darkness; Josiah would register her presence and he would sound like his old self when he'd finally reply.

"I'm okay now. . . . Is there water?" Dagg would hold his head while he sipped tepid water from a hospital straw. "OK . . ." he'd say again. "It's nighttime . . . go to sleep now."

But Dagg could not sleep; it felt too much like keeping vigil, and perhaps because of how many nights others had failed her, she wanted more than anything not to fail Josiah now. At three she got up and walked the dim halls of the fourth floor. Night nurses and orderlies watched her suspiciously as if she'd come to do some harm. At three-twenty she lay down again, staring out the window toward the phosphorus sky. It was raining a light slow drizzle, and the low thick clouds reflected back the orange pink of the street lights. Josiah thrashed and moaned and called out to someone. "It's OK," Dagg said. "It's all OK now." She didn't know why she said those things, but the words did soothe him. She was discovering that anything soothed him; the important thing was the sound of her voice.

"Are we ready for this?" Josiah sat up in bed and looked over at her patiently. He sounded so normal and conversational that it was hard to remember he was out of his mind.

"We're ready, Josiah. . . . I think we're ready." He seemed almost to smile at her a moment and then lay down again. His breathing softened into sleep almost instantly, and he didn't wake again until the first nurse bustled in when shifts changed in the morning.

Dagg stumbled out of the just-waking hospital sometime before six. It was still dark over the city, but looking east Dagg could see a line of first dawn just beyond the Cascade Mountains. She drove home in a daze, let herself in quietly, stripped off her clothing in the bathroom and showered, then slipped naked into bed next to Patrice, whose body felt so wonderfully warm and full and alive. Dagg kissed her back and shoulders and hugged her body closer until Patrice moaned and turned over, opening her arms to let Dagg in. They made love in a kind of half-sleep, murmuring to each other in groggy voices, and after coming together, both fell back into a deep sleep and didn't wake again until almost nine.

Dagg woke to the rare feel of sunlight streaming in across the bed. She threw back her side of the covers and lay soaking up the warmth for awhile before stretching and stumbling to the kitchen to put water on for coffee. When she came back into the bedroom Patrice was sitting up, looking sleepy and disheveled. Dagg handed her an extra bed pillow, placed two against the headboard on her own side, and brought in two mugs of coffee.

Patrice sipped her coffee and moaned, contented. "How was Josiah last night?"

"Somewhere . . . he's somewhere else mostly. I think it's OK though."

"He's dying, isn't he?"

Dagg nodded. "But, wherever he goes on the way there, I think it's good. It's not too scary. There's a place beside death; it's the place of our memories, where we put the things we can't bear to remember, or the parts of ourselves we can't stand to be. Death walks by there . . . or we

do. We pass through that room again on the way to our dying. I was
there . . . in that room last night with Josiah. We spent the night in
the room I could never go in. Only it was different. I'm an adult now,
and I could love Josiah and make him not so afraid of that place."
Dagg balanced her mug on her raised knee, watching the steam rise
up and catch dust motes in the sunlight. "Josiah is good; he's good to
the core. Consciousness peels away and beneath it he's still sweet-
ness." She set her coffee carefully on the night table and folded both
arms behind her head. "It won't be true for me, Patrice, I warn you."

Patrice laughed. "I know that!"

"I have this rage at the core . . . the oldest rage. I'm afraid when
consciousness peels away I'll kill somebody."

"Shall I wake Zach?" Patrice swung her legs off of the bed and began to stand up, but Dagg grabbed her elbow and pulled her back on
the bed. "Wait a minute." Dagg crossed her legs and faced Patrice, releasing her grip on Patrice's arm so that she could sit up. "I slept with
someone else—a woman in Tacoma." Dagg watched Patrice carefully, waiting for a reaction.

Patrice exhaled loudly. "That was it then. . . . I knew something
was different . . . and so . . . that was it."

"I don't know why."

"Do you still want her?"

"I didn't even want her then!"

Patrice started to laugh and then, noticing the stricken expression
on her partner's face, laughed even louder. "You're supposed to at
least *want* the people you sleep with."

"I know, but it was something else really I wanted. I wanted power . . .
the power to make her want *me* . . . or I wanted . . . I don't know . . .
something that wasn't her but maybe I could get for a minute."

Patrice lay back down, pulling a sheet over her legs and stomach.
"What is it you really want?"

Dagg looked surprised, not by the question but because hearing it,
she so clearly knew the answer. "I want that love I can never remember the name of . . . that kind where someone loves you no matter
what you do or think or say. I want a family . . . people who stay no

matter what happens. I want a family and I have you and Josiah and Zach."

"That is a family."

"Where's the picket fence then? Where's the . . .?" Dagg looked desperately around the bedroom as if the thing she was lacking might be spotted there. "I want people who stay. And Josiah is dying and you are always half out the door."

"I'm not. . . . I swear it. . . . I will stay."

"And stay alive." Dagg slammed her empty cup onto the table. "I don't want numb dead people around me, and . . . I don't want to be all numb myself."

"So you had an affair." Patrice started laughing.

Dagg slumped down on the bed. "I just wanted the picket fence. I didn't want to hurt you, Patrice."

"You didn't hurt me."

Dagg threw a pillow at her legs. "Well, you know I wanted to."

"I know that. I'm just grateful for once something isn't my fault."

The sun disappeared behind clouds by eleven that morning, and by the time Dagg dressed and drove to the hospital a light drizzle had become a slow steady torrent of rain. Josiah's hospital room was packed with people: two nurses, a lab tech drawing blood samples, and a respiratory technician, a young fat guy with pudgy soft fingers who'd thrown Josiah against his shoulder and was tapping on his back with a soft rubber mallet.

"Yes, I am receiving visitors . . ." Josiah smiled at her from the short arms of the respiratory tech, looking more like himself and less for an instant like a gigantic starving baby.

"You're looking better today, Josiah." Dagg squeezed his foot at the bottom of the bed, because the crowd working around him made it impossible to get any closer.

"They've been giving me oxygen." Josiah waved upward to a large green translucent mask descending toward his mouth and nose. The respiratory tech explained to Dagg and to Josiah that it was crucial that Josiah leave that face mask on. When the group had finally left them and moved on to the room next door, Josiah lifted the mask and rested it high on his forehead until he looked like a mad scientist just out of the lab for a breath of fresh air.

"Leave it on, please, Josiah."

He smiled at her kindly, and Dagg was struck by something Patrice had said that morning—she said the brain was like an onion, with personality and reason on the outermost layers. The nurses insisted on "orienting" Josiah—telling him in strong firm voices that he was in the hospital and the green mask on his nose would help get enough oxygen to his brain—but it seemed to Dagg he was happier in that other place he drifted to, and while Josiah's consciousness peeled away, he was a kind man to the core.

Even out of his mind he was polite to the nurses, even in his ravings he was gentle and funny. Dagg had assumed that beneath our good manners and social behavior all of us were built on a rock-hard core of rage. It occurred to her now that the rage was hers only, and when her outer onion peeled away, there would be no smiles and politeness, just that rock-hard core of rage. She pulled the mask gently back into place over Josiah's nose and mouth. "Leave it, Josiah," she said quietly. "It makes you look like a cricket."

He rolled his eyes theatrically. "Everything with you is about insects."

"What?"

"Didn't you sleep in here last night?"

"I did, Josiah."

He nodded and his eyes drifted closed; he seemed to sleep for a moment and then opened them again. "The room was so full then . . . everyone has so many people."

Patrice had ordered a bouquet of flowers from a downtown florist. It always amazed Dagg that Patrice came from a world where people thought of things like that. The floral arrangement was massive: blue columbine and orange and yellow daisies surrounding three giant sprays of bird-of-paradise. Josiah stared at the flowers on the table at the foot of his bed. "I keep looking and looking at those flowers. A flower is a miracle, don't you think?"

Dagg sat down next to his bed and rested her feet on the bed rail. "They're pretty, Josiah. Did you want the TV on?" Above them three hysterical women vied for a sports car on *The Price Is Right*.

Josiah glanced up at it, looking confused. "I've been trying to avoid it, but I think the nurses keep turning it on." Dagg found the remote wrapped around the rail of his bed and, after fumbling with the un-marked buttons, managed finally to turn off the TV. "It's raining, isn't it?" Josiah stared out the window toward the matte gray sky and soft rain.

"Just drizzling."

"Open the window, I want to smell it. I think I saw the sun this morning."

Dagg pushed open the window, and the room filled with the sweet-ness of rain and with the sound of traffic on wet streets. Josiah breathed deeply, unaware that the oxygen mask was in place, and perhaps the smell of rain did enter, because it seemed to relax him and he soon fell asleep.

A nurse came in an hour later and turned the TV back on. "It helps," she whispered to Dagg, "to keep patients oriented."

"Oriented to what?" Dagg looked up at the TV: a woman in an evening gown lounged across a luxury car for sale.

"Life." The woman smiled happily, as if just that sort of thing was the hospital's specialty. Dagg nodded and waited in the hallway while the woman changed Josiah's IV, gave him a sponge bath, and changed his sheets.

When Dagg came back into the room Josiah was awake again, but exhausted, as if all that attention had worn him back down. "Life," he said, pointing toward the television. On screen two young actresses in a soap opera were screaming at each other without sound. Dagg laughed and clicked the thing off again—it was so weird, what Josiah heard and what slipped past him.

Zach

I

Josiah was dying. Zach heard Dagg and his mom say the words to each other, but they bumped into a wall his brain made, flowed out from him, and lost their meaning. It was too close and stale in the hospital room, too stuffy and antiseptic smelling. Zach glanced toward Josiah's inert form on the bed—his face was pasty white against the pillow, his thin wasted body seemed lost beneath the sheet. Josiah was dying, that's what his mom said, but Zach couldn't feel anything but the overwhelming desire to run away. There was something metallic and stiff around his chest now, a kind of smothering constriction even to his heart.

At home or at school Zach felt a terrible impatience to get back to the hospital, as if something was happening there and he wanted in. But after running to catch the Broadway bus to get there again, he found upon entering the hospital room that the same terrible constriction was back. He paced from the door to the open window, then turned and paced back to the empty spare bed where his mother lay watching the small, soundless television on the wall above their heads. Dagg stretched out in the armchair leafing through a magazine and watching Josiah's chest rise and fall.

Zach turned back to the open door and stared out into the hall. He couldn't think about Josiah; he was trying too hard to stand still, to not run. He walked back to the open window and stared down into the parking lot four floors below. Josiah coughed; the bed rail rattled. Zach rushed back to the open door, stopping before the sink at the sound of his mother's voice as she rose and whispered something to Josiah, straightened his blanket, and offered him a sip of water. Zach stared at himself in the small round mirror above the sink—his eyes looked round and enormous, and afraid.

Josiah coughed again, and Dagg stood up to see what he needed. She glanced across the room at Zach as if his pacing annoyed her. Josiah said something unintelligible and tried to sit upright. The movement pulled his sheet loose and exposed one bony blue-white foot at the bottom of the bed. Zach stared at the foot, afraid of it; the foot looked blue and cold and dead already, as if death had entered through Josiah's foot and was now making its way upward.

Patrice and Dagg straightened the blanket and sheet, tucking in the foot, which disappeared from sight. Josiah opened his eyes and looked at Zach, who could barely look back. "Hospitals scare him," Josiah said to Patrice. He lifted the thin plastic tube to his oxygen mask and stared at it. "Send him along—this is nothing for a boy to see."

Patrice motioned for Zach to leave if he wanted, and Zach bolted from the room, half ran down the long hospital hallway, and propelled himself headlong through the half empty lobby.

Outside he stopped, bent over in the small square of lawn that fronted the hospital. He rested his hands on his knees and breathed again, slowly and deeply, trying to remember when he'd first held his breath. He straightened slowly to discover his mom watching him from the open hospital door. She stood on the electric pad outside the door, staring at him, seemingly oblivious to the alarm's constant buzzing. Finally she stepped forward and the door closed behind her. She walked down the sidewalk to the patch of lawn and lay one open hand along Zach's back.

"You OK?"

Zach nodded. She draped one arm across his heaving shoulders and propelled them back to the sidewalk and down the street, away from the hospital and the rush of traffic, to a small side street that led off Broadway and into a residential part of the Hill. At the feel of her hand on him and the pressure of her gentle direction, Zach surrendered and followed gratefully, but he couldn't will himself to look at her and kept his head ducked and his eyes on the sidewalk.

They walked two blocks east to a coffee shop on a quiet street corner, a small art deco storefront with six small tables on the sidewalk out front. Zach ordered a cheeseburger, fries, and a chocolate malted milkshake; his mom ordered coffee and drank it turned away from him, as if she was waiting for someone who would be walking down that street.

She was beautiful, his mother. He had always known that. Her blunt-cut blonde hair framed her face like a gentle soft hat. Her cheekbones and jaw seemed so fragile and delicate, not at all like the thick, broad bones of his face.

"Josiah is dying." His mom said the words so quietly Zach had to strain to hear them. She moved her chair toward him and rested one delicate hand on his arm. "This time we spend with him is the last time. I don't want you to miss it, and maybe you'll regret that later."

"I can't breathe in that room." Zach felt his chest constrict even to say it. He looked away from his mother, first to the empty plates littering the table, and then away down the street. Patrice paid the bill and took his arm again, walking them farther away from Broadway, past shade-covered Victorian houses, which sat looking peaceful and stately under massive elm trees.

"I know that feeling . . . that you can't breathe."

Zach tried to pull away at her words, but his mom tucked his arm beneath hers and pressed him to her side. "Don't pull. Listen, Zach. What I missed, when I left you, I can't ever have that back. I left you when you needed me. I left a little boy and came home to find a young man. There won't ever be a second chance. I can't ever fix that thing I lost."

She stopped walking and turned to face him, placing her open palm on the side of his cheek. Zach looked down at the cracks in the sidewalk; he didn't want to breathe or look at her now. On the sidewalk his heavy work boots faced off against her delicate green fabric shoes. She touched his chin and tilted his face up. "I was wrong to miss any part of love—even the most hurtful."

She released his chin, and Zach began to walk slowly. She fell into step beside him and tucked her arm through his like a girl on a date.

"Dagg shared with you something I couldn't. I feel guilty about what you lost, but I feel some envy too."

Zach tried to pull his arm free, but again his mother stopped him. "I'm not trying to get that right, Zach. I'm saying that I don't want you to miss it—these last times with Josiah. It won't spare you any hurt, whether or not you decide you can stay."

"I can't breathe in there—it's not a decision."

Patrice laughed, releasing his arm and turning back toward the hospital. "Yeah, I know, it feels like it's not a decision, but trust me, it is. It really is, Zach."

Raul sprawled across a worn armchair in the waiting room reading *People* magazine. He jumped up when he saw them approaching, then seemed confused by his own action and sat back down again. Patrice held out her hand to pull the boy upright, saying that Josiah would be happy to see him.

Josiah was totally out of his mind now—or at least out of his mind as they had known it. The boys entered the room to find him sitting on the edge of his bed fumbling with the hose of his oxygen mask. He smiled at them gently. "If you had a knife, we could cut this loose."

Zach looked stricken and froze in place, but Dagg took the cord from Josiah and said maybe they could cut it later. "And who is this boy?" Josiah smiled at Raul. "Are you from the room with all those boxes?"

"It's Raul. Remember Raul?" Dagg smiled at the frightened boy and motioned for him to find a chair. Raul sat cautiously on the edge of the spare bed, looking as if at any moment he might bolt to the door. Zach balled one fist into his cheekbone, rubbing the soft part of his cheek with one hand. Dagg led him from the room and motioned for Raul to stay with Josiah. Raul looked panicked at the thought of it but moved to a chair just a bit closer, while Dagg led Zach to a set of chairs at the end of the long hall.

"He is dying, isn't he?" Zach rushed the words out, then bit down, clamping his jaw as if not to cry.

Dagg nodded, wrapping her arms around his neck. At the touch of her hands Zach sank against her shoulder. Dagg gently pushed him upright and wiped his tear-streaked face with her hand. "If there is anything left you need to say to Josiah, I think you'd better say it now."

The boy nodded, close to tears again, then slowly rose and walked back to the hospital room. "Josiah!" he called softly, but the man seemed deep in sleep again. "He can't hear me!" Zach cried out, and the tone of his voice sent Raul fleeing back down the hall.

"Just tell him," Dagg said. "We don't really know what he hears."

Zach pulled a chair close to the bed and began to whisper intently to Josiah. He looked like a penitent bowed before a priest. Zach took hold of Josiah's hand. "I don't want . . . I don't want you to go!" He started to cry again, resting his head on the other man's chest, and as he wept he felt Josiah's hand come up and begin to pat his shoulder.

"Please don't go, Josiah! Please don't!" The boy was crying so hard now that the whole bed shook; his racking sobs made the metal bed rails rattle. Josiah opened his eyes slowly and looked down at the boy. He seemed about to say something but then started coughing. "Dear God . . . don't let him die . . . don't let him!" Zach didn't know where he got the idea that there might be a God somewhere who cared about them. He stopped crying, finally, and lay still against Josiah's chest. Through the thin hospital blanket he could just hear a heartbeat. Josiah was leaving; he was just that faint heartbeat from gone. Soon it would halt and all would be silence. Zach sat up again and took hold of the older man's hand. "Josiah . . . I'm sorry I ever . . . anything. . . . I love you so much!" The boy began to cry again, shaking and sobbing, and at first he didn't notice the pressure of Josiah's fingers.

Josiah's eyes opened, and he reached up shakily and pushed up the oxygen mask, then took Zach's hand and just held it, staring at his face, so patient and gentle and loving and kind. Zach wiped his eyes and sniffed back his tears. He looked at Josiah, who seemed suddenly ancient and frail, looking not like his friend but like a gray-faced old man. "I will miss you," Zach said simply.

Josiah smiled gently and Zach felt a light pressure against his fingers, as if Josiah was trying to squeeze his hand. "Madagascar against South Africa . . . I am attacking with twenty-six armies." Josiah grinned happily past Zach, and the boy knew they were not here now; they were meeting again on a happier day.

"You win, Josiah . . . you win." Zach bent over slowly to kiss Josiah's cheek, then pulled the green oxygen mask back down on his face. "Just breathe . . . okay . . . just keep breathing." Zach lay next to Josiah along the narrow strip of bed, feeling the rise and fall of Josiah's chest under his hand. After another fifteen minutes Josiah tried to sit up and fumbled at the mask, pulling it down so that it clung below his chin. Dagg and Raul came back into the room and Josiah looked at them, suddenly confused and worried. "Something is happening to me," he said.

Zach started crying again and Dagg led him from the room, motioning to Raul to please stay a moment. Raul swallowed and edged toward the bed; if they had not been just outside blocking the doorway, he might well have bolted. "Zach?" Josiah sat up, looking around the room.

Raul edged closer to him. "It's only me . . . Raul."

Josiah reached out, grabbed the boy's arm, and pulled himself toward him; then with one arm on the boy for balance he placed his other palm flat on Raul's forehead. "Oh Lord," he said in a loud voice, "let him learn the lessons he needs to learn in life without hurting other people!" Josiah released the boy and fell back onto the bed, and Raul turned and called to Zach. "He said . . . I think what he said . . . he meant that for you." Raul placed his own palm on Zach's forehead. "He thought . . . he thought I was you."

On the bed Josiah murmured something and once again pulled down at his mask. A nurse entered the room, readjusted it, and frowned at them all like they were letting her down.

"I need a cigarette." Raul released Zach's arm and walked down the hallway. Dagg motioned to Zach that she would sit with Josiah if he wanted to go now. Zach stared for the last time at his sleeping friend, then turned and followed Raul down the hall.

Josiah died that night while Patrice, Dagg, and Zach were sleeping, scattered about the hospital room on the spare bed and empty

chairs. Sometime before dawn Dagg woke suddenly, disturbed perhaps by the sudden silence. Her jerking movements on the bed woke
Patrice, and she reached out to Zach and gently woke him up. They
buzzed for the night nurse and waited, staring in shock at Josiah's
now-lifeless form. "Why'd he die when we were sleeping?" Zach
glanced at his mother, afraid perhaps that he'd let his friend down.

Patrice stroked his arm. "People do. They die mostly in the night,
and they mostly die alone."

"We should have stayed awake with him," Zach said.

Patrice touched his arm. "It was time for him—that's why he looks
peaceful."

Zach wrenched his arm from her grasp. "He doesn't look peaceful;
he looks dead." He watched as the night nurse straightened Josiah's
body on the cold bed and placed a rolled hospital towel beneath his
chin. Josiah looked still and cold in the pale morning light—so waxy
and empty—so unlike himself.

II

Josiah's will left everything he had to Zach: a ten-thousand-dollar
insurance policy, his Valiant, everything in his apartment, and his
video store. He was cremated according to his wishes, and Dagg,
Patrice, and Zach rode the ferry to Winslow one Saturday morning
and scattered his ashes out beyond the shipping channel.

It took three months to finish probate and make all Josiah's pay-
ments to his various creditors. In the end, Patrice and Dagg had to
borrow against the video store in order to pay off hospital bills and the
last of his debts. Dagg sold her greyhound game concession, making
just enough money to pay the MasterCard bill. This made her bank
either so delighted or so sad that they raised her credit limit another
two thousand dollars. She requested a new gold card inscribed *Dagger
Wyatt: Sword Swallower.* The bank happily acquiesced, welcoming her
once again to their family of customers.

Friends helped them clear out Josiah's apartment. Zach kept Josiah's
cane and his VCR; everything else was sorted and thrown away, given
to friends, or donated to the Orion Center. As much as Zach had loved

Josiah, he felt almost nothing for the things Josiah had left him. Only the smell of Josiah was precious in them—only the memory of his thin pale hands on his thick plastic mugs.

Patrice suggested that Zach might want to keep Josiah's china, because he would need things like that for his own place someday. But Josiah's china meant nothing to Zach. He kept only the two plastic mugs in which Josiah had always served their pop. The good china held no memories; it was the cheap plastic mugs that reminded Zach most of his friend.

Maya arranged a memorial service to be held on June first in Volunteer Park. All Josiah's friends were there, and many old customers, Frank McKinny and the staff of the Orion Center, the Kitchen Angels, half the Gay Men's Network, and even Raul. As people sang and prayed and told funny stories, Zach was struck by the strangest part of death: not only was there no more of Josiah, but there were now a forever limited number of stories. The stories felt so precious to him that Zach wanted to soak each one up; each one became another moment Josiah lived again.

Zach listened and laughed but said nothing. He felt that he should have a story to share, but he didn't. He had only pictures in him now, pictures of Josiah on the living room floor or sprawled across the couch, Josiah walking beside him awkwardly, his arms and legs like a strange fierce beetle. Zach had the terrifying images of Josiah in his hospital bed playing with the oxygen hose. He'd looked less like a man Zach knew then and sadly like an aging cricket. Zach carried the last image of Josiah as well: gray-still with death and waxy, a hospital towel stuffed under his chin. It was this image Zach most wanted to run from, but no matter what he did he could not escape it. It haunted that space between waking and sleep.

There were pictures, endless pictures: Zach listened and absorbed each new story, but he couldn't find his own to tell. He had never been a talker; he couldn't explain the world in words. There were only the endless shifting visual memories; there were now only the still-life pictures. Maya hugged him after the memorial and asked if there was anything she could do. Zach shook his head and thanked her, noticing he was now as tall as she was.

At home that next week Zach wandered in a trance throughout the apartment. He kept staring at the place on the floor where Josiah once sprawled to play Risk with him, and he missed his friend most of all in those moments, knowing, as he stared at the empty place on the floor, the complete and final absence of Josiah from his life.

The Orion Center program ended on June 12, a week after school let out for the year. Zach helped Frank McKinny lock up for the summer, and they walked downtown together and bought fish and chips on the waterfront below the ferry docks. They sat outside on a pier over the water, eating and throwing french fries to the hovering seagulls.

"You miss him, don't you lad?" McKinny stood with his back to the picnic table, looking out across the bay.

Zach nodded. "Yeah." He said the word flatly, almost like a breath.

McKinny threw another french fry up over the edge of the pier and a seagull dove for it, catching a piece of it while the rest fell into the bay below. "Other cultures have such meaningful rites for their mourning; here we throw a cocktail party. We're embarrassed if anyone really expresses sorrow."

"I'm OK," Zach said.

"Of course you're OK. But the question I'm asking is, What will you do with your friend, Josiah? What will you do yourself to mourn him?"

"I'm OK."

McKinny hurrumphed and finished his fried fish. "You think that makes you more a man, so stoic that your friend is gone?"

Zach looked at Frank McKinny blankly. He didn't know the words to say how completely his sorrow lived only in pictures, how much he missed Josiah and how alone he felt without him.

McKinny stared out over the water. "The joyful will stoop with sorrow, and when you have gone to the earth I will let my hair grow long for your sake. . . ." He declaimed the line with a stage actor's air, then collapsed into himself again and turned back to Zach. "A man named Gilganesh said that. He wasn't afraid to feel so much for his friend."

Zach threw his paper plate and napkins away and started back up the pier toward the street. He felt angry and ashamed and confused, as if McKinny thought he didn't love Josiah, didn't love him right somehow. McKinny caught up with him in front of the chips stand, but Zach turned away. "I have to get home now."

"I know how much you loved him, Zach."

"There are no . . ." Zach stopped, confused by what he wanted to say. "It's not like in a play where people have the words they need."

"Words?" McKinny looked like something suddenly became clear for him. "Is it words you've been struggling with?"

"I . . . get . . . just pictures . . . then sometimes smells, but mostly pictures."

McKinny put his arm over Zach's shoulders and walked him to the bus stop. "Then use the pictures in your head . . . a picture can hold everything. A picture can hold whatever you need."

So Zach began to draw pictures. He bought himself a drawing tablet and drew portraits of Josiah. Josiah laughing on the floor beside him. Josiah angry with his cane, towering above him in the small living room. He filled the tablet with Josiah and then bought another. In this tablet went also self-portraits drawn while staring in the mirror, portraits of Dagg behind the counter of her greyhound game, portraits of Patrice, McKinny, and Raul. His mom and Dagg often asked to see his pictures, or asked what he was drawing, but Zach would close his tablet quickly and not be able to answer them. He didn't know how to say he was filling the tablets with his life.

III

It was Maya who first suggested Zach make a panel for the AIDS Memorial Quilt. When Patrice had come to the Orion Center to sign the boy's court release form she had mentioned Zach's new passion with the drawing pad, and Maya had given them the number of the NAMES Project—the people responsible for making the quilt.

Zach cut bright blue and yellow and red and green continents out of wool felt and made a panel with the world on it—a giant Risk game in progress, because he wanted most to hold the memory of Josiah on the floor all those nights beside him; Josiah attacking Madagascar with twenty-six armies.

Patrice and Dagg had both helped with the sewing, and Maya embroidered the border with bright yellow thread. The panel wasn't a speech and it wasn't a story, but everything Zach felt about Josiah somehow ended up inside it.

Patrice drove him to the NAMES Project office to drop off his finished panel. The NAMES Project occupied a small storefront on the south end of Broadway between the KFC and the Unity Church. The space had been a dry cleaner's once, and the small dark room still smelled vaguely of cleaning solvent and soiled clothes, in spite of the total renovation into a quilt-making factory. The dry cleaner's front counter had been left in place, and it was here Zach carefully unfolded Josiah's finished panel as the people working in the back all came forward to admire it. He and Patrice stretched the panel tight between them, and Zach haltingly tried to tell about it, although the words mostly failed him and he said only that it was a game he and Josiah used to play.

The entire quilt was set for display in Washington, DC, in early October, but the deadline for new panels had already passed. The project was so enormous (the quilt was already eighteen acres) that they couldn't get new panels into it in time for the quilt to be packed in San Francisco and shipped east in railroad cars. "We'll hang it here in the shop for now," the woman working at the counter told him. "It will still be part of our local displays."

Zach nodded, setting his end down on the counter, but Patrice held on to her end and asked, "Isn't there any way to get this in? The display isn't for another three months."

"There's a booth they're setting up when the quilt is displayed there. New panels can be brought in then. They'll lay them in a special section."

Zach looked at his mother anxiously. She folded the panel with the stranger's help and set it on the counter. "Hang it for now," she said, taking Zach by the shoulder. "But we'll be back in October; we'll take it to the quilt ourselves."

They left the shop and walked up Broadway toward their car. Patrice asked him if he wanted lunch while they were out. They went to Shoko Café, a small sushi bar on the north end of the hill, and

Patrice ate California rolls and sweet shrimp while Zach ate shrimp tempura.

"Are we really driving to Washington?" Zach looked at his mother expectantly. He half expected that she'd been lying.

"Why not, Zach? Why not? You made that for Josiah, and I want it to be part of the whole quilt—the whole, enormous, monstrous quilt that even the president might come to look at."

The president would see it—Josiah's Risk panel—for some reason the thought made Zach especially happy. The president himself would know then how important and special Josiah had been. Zach imagined the president staring down at Josiah's colorful panel. "There," Zach would say, as if that explained everything. "Now you know it."

IV

That summer Zach worked half days and all day Saturdays at the video store, then spent his afternoons and evenings hanging around the Orion House. The theater program was closed down for the summer and McKinny was off somewhere on a bender, but Meryl Danner's drawing class still met three afternoons a week, and Zach had forced himself to sign up.

The class met in a large, messy Orion House classroom, which was perfect for drawing class because its large bank of windows let in so much northern light. Zach was shy about his drawing; the others seemed so sure about it. He sat in the back of the room in one corner, where he could prop his chair against the back wall and no one could walk behind him to peer over his shoulder.

The model for that Friday was an athletic-looking girl with freckled, pale skin and coppery hair that fell past her shoulders. Aria was a year older than Zach and went to high school at Baker Hill, where, she said laughingly, she majored in track. She posed in her track clothes today; her arms and legs rippled with long smooth muscles under fair, freckled skin.

It was hard to draw the human body; hands, arms, and legs were especially difficult. Zach began and discarded three different beginnings before finding some lines on the page that seemed honest to him. He drew intently for over two hours, not even breaking when the model rested, but using those moments to shade and catch up. When the class was finally over at seven, Aria stretched, put on her warm-ups, and walked back to his corner, wanting to see what Zach had drawn.

Zach closed his sketch pad, startled by her appearance at his left shoulder. Her smell up close was strange to him—an unnerving mixture of fresh sweat and soap. "It's nothing. I'm not really—a draw-er, I mean, an artist. I just like to try it, but the body is the hardest." Zach looked at her face: her small upturned nose, blue eyes so intent on him. "The legs and arms are hard—the length and dimension, to be honest about muscles, how you can see them even though they're under skin." He stopped, mortified that he'd even said this. Weren't guys supposed to say other kinds of things to girls?

"I'd like to see it. I know you draw well." She looked a little scared herself now. "Raul showed me some pictures you made of your friend."

Raul had showed her? Zach grabbed his jean jacket and tossed his pencils and erasers into a small plastic box. "I have to—"

"Can I walk with you? We catch the same bus to Fremont, you know."

He didn't know, but now she told him. They'd been riding the same bus home from the center every day. How had he not noticed? Well, she wore more clothes on the bus, for one thing. Had she still been in her running shorts he would have recognized the muscles in her legs. They walked to the bus stop and waited awkwardly together. She was a year older than he was and almost as tall.

"What kind of name is Aria?"

She laughed, looking embarrassed. "My mother thought of it. She wanted to be an opera singer, but she wasn't really good enough."

Zach shoved his hands into his jeans pockets and stared down Rainier Avenue as if searching for the bus.

"What kind of name is Zach?"

"My name. My mother . . ." He didn't know where it came from. "I guess my mother liked the name."

Aria stretched her head back as if her muscles were stiff from posing. "It's a good name. Clean. It makes me think you're honest."

Honest? Zach imagined being honest. How exactly did an honest Zach behave? They rode together to his stop on Stone Way. Zach said good-bye and started to the front of the bus. "Zach," she said quietly. "Call me." He stopped. "Call me and someday show me your pictures."

That night Zach lay awake long after his mother and Dagg had turned out the lights. He imagined calling Aria and what he would say. He opened the sketch pad on his dresser and turned to the day's drawings—how could he show them to the girl? How could he let her see he'd been drawing her naked?

Dagg

Dagg and Zach worked the early shift in the video store that summer, then Patrice and Raul worked until closing. Hiring Raul had been Zach's only demand as the store's official in-trust owner. His friend was saving money to get his own apartment, and Zach had insisted, in spite of their doubts, that Raul be given a job there. Patrice had been especially against it but had acquiesced at Zach's insistence, and after a month of double checking Raul's cash receipts and figures, finally acknowledged he hadn't stolen from them yet.

Dagg turned over the cash register at five and walked home through a beautiful balmy summer evening, finding that once she arrived at the house she couldn't bear to go in yet. It was too beautiful outside that evening; the sun was still high and warm in the sky, and the city felt freshened by light offshore breezes. Dagg caught a bus that ran down Eastlake and got off in front of the Eastlake Grill. She found a table out back on the deck overlooking Lake Union and ordered a roast beef sandwich with horseradish sauce, potato salad, and an Anchor Steam Beer. The air smelled salty and fresh like the ocean, mixed slightly with the smell of diesel fumes and motor oil. Small boats roared up and down the lake and from the restaurant she could see where small seaplanes took off and landed. Dagg especially loved watching the seaplanes; they made life seem lighter and less consequential, as if it wasn't hard to do, all that coming and going.

"Dagg?" Someone touched her shoulder. She looked up into the vaguely familiar face of Carol Stark.

"Carol?" It really was a question, for the woman looked different to her now. Relaxed and smiling, suntanned and healthy.

"Can I join you for a minute?" Carol touched the back of the empty chair.

"Sure." Dagg straightened, unsure what to say next and confused by what she didn't feel. The woman seemed like a stranger to her. She was a stranger, and yet they had made love one night. Dagg remembered the musty smell of cigarettes and the chill of the woman's unheated bedroom; the memory made her feel lonely and sad. Carol sat staring at her, waiting for her to say something.

"You look . . . suntanned," Dagg said finally. "How did you manage that in Tacoma?"

Carol laughed; the sound fluttered up and down in her like the trill of a flute. Dagg wondered why she didn't remember that, then realized that she'd never heard it. "I've been in California." Carol touched her hair. "I quit my job and sold my house. I spent the last three months at the beach."

Carol ordered a beer, and they talked for an hour. Dagg didn't register much of it, only that the woman had changed; that Carol seemed relaxed and happy.

"People change," Carol said when Dagg mentioned it. Dagg had wanted to say, *They do not.*

At home Dagg slowly filled the bathtub and stared at her too-earnest face in the steamy mirror. "You're married, not dead," she said to her reflection. Fine lines creased the sides of her eyes; she tried to erase them with the tip of her finger. "You're not dead yet," she repeated.

From Zach's bedroom she heard the rippling sound of Aria's laughter, followed a split second later by the deep happy rumble of her son. They sounded so innocent, so happy together; had she ever felt something so pure for Patrice?

People did leave. It was always in darkness. They released the last strands of love and drifted free of themselves. Her mother had. It had been so simple. Just a slight folding of the tent flap and her mother had slipped free. Whatever love was it was certainly heavy; like carrying luggage through an airport for the rest of your life. She loved Patrice as much as she could love. Now, with the long winter just behind her, that didn't feel like much. Maybe love was like the Wheel of

Life game Gazelle had once run—number seventeen promised a Hawaii vacation, but the pin had been shaved slightly and the wheel would never stop there, no matter how careful or lucky you got.

Her mother had packed her bags for love—walked off to find it. The tent flap had waved open; her mother had slipped away in the night. Dagg sat back in the hot bath and stared at the steamy bathroom window. Even in remembering, a small, high noise still rose from her throat. Her mother freezes at the sound, but she'll never turn back.

From Zach's bedroom, the laughter faded into an ominous and lingering silence. Dagg dried off from her bath, wrapped a cotton robe around herself, and knocked once on his door before looking in. The kids startled back from an embrace, embarrassed and flustered. Their overheated faces made Dagg want to smile.

"Do you mind?" Zach stood up to close his bedroom door, but Dagg put her hand out and stopped it.

"I do mind. Keep your door open when Aria's here."

"Why?"

Because you care about her, Zach. Because you don't want her life to go faster than the child can live with. Those weren't words that she could say to Zach or that he could hear now. "Because I said so!" Dagg sounded stuffy and rigid, even to herself.

That summer she had watched Zach grow and grow away from them. He was drifting away toward his own adulthood, and that was as it should be, wasn't it? He worked his shifts at the video store and spent the rest of the time drawing, or else with his new girlfriend, or talking to her on the phone. It amazed Dagg that the boy could spend six hours with his girlfriend, then come home and immediately call her.

Should they be talking to him about birth control? About sexually transmitted diseases? Aria, although a year older than Zach, seemed so young and innocent. Was it their job to protect her from the possibly wolfish intent of their son? Yet Zach didn't seem wolfish—he seemed fourteen and happy that summer. Perhaps it was enough, to love him for now and leave him alone.

She and Patrice were adults; they had chosen each other. They had no one but themselves to run from. Dagg could not make herself believe it—the old myth some people seemed to have that you could be a better person by getting yourself to a different, better place. Patrice had failed her, failed Zach—the words seemed like bad lines from a melodrama now. Patrice was just Patrice, after all. She loved them both the best she knew how. And a cellophane heart was its own form of strange betrayal—Dagg had nothing more to offer than her own resentful decision to stay. Well, she wanted to stay; she thought she could now. She could stay with Patrice and try to love her. She would try to love her as well as she could. Dagg wanted to believe she had learned *something* from Ammachi—that love is something given, not something won or earned. What kind of love had Ammachi talked about? Dagg tried to remember the word *unconditional,* but she could never think of that word and always came up with *unrequited* instead.

But she would stay, for now. She would stay. After Zach went to walk Aria back to the bus stop, Dagg poured herself a glass of water and sprawled on the couch in the darkened living room, watching the shadows of headlights drift across the walls. In memory she heard her old friend Chinaco. They were sitting again in his sunlit kitchen. Dagger was eating Oreos and Chinaco was sipping a glass of red wine. "God sends us the people we are to love," he said. "And so in gratitude if nothing else, we should find in ourselves the faith to love them."

On the third Wednesday in October, Dagg sat on the bed watching Patrice pack for her trip to the AIDS Memorial Quilt. Patrice folded a blouse and placed it in the open suitcase, then turned and pulled a sweater and a jacket from the closet behind her. They had already discussed the business arrangements for the week, and they had gone over the schedule for the video store. Now Patrice placed the last of her clothes into the suitcase and pushed down on the lid to fasten the clasps. Dagg watched as she set the suitcase into the hall outside the bedroom, then swung her legs off of the bed. "Do you believe people change? Do you believe that, Patrice?"

Patrice looked startled. "Into what, Dagg?"

"I ran into someone recently—a woman I once knew. And she said, 'People change,' and I wanted to say, 'They do not.'"

"Do you mind that you're not going? Did you want to go with us?"

Dagg shook her head and stood up from the bed. She was glad to stay home and have something be ordinary—to not do this necessary thing and have it still get done. Patrice pushed Dagg back onto the bed and then lay down next to her, resting her head against Dagg's shoulder. Sunlight streamed in through the bedroom window, casting horizontal bands across the middle of their thighs. Dagg reached down toward the band of light, letting her fingers try to grasp the dust motes that touched down against her outstretched fingers.

"Do you remember when we met, Dagg? That first morning we met on the beach?" Patrice reached down to Dagg's hand and pulled it upward, touching the open palm against the corner of her mouth. "Did you want me then—that first morning? Did you want me the first time we met?"

Dagg looked down at Patrice's face, trying to remember that first morning. "I thought Zach was dear," she said finally. "Zach was dear and you annoyed me."

Patrice laughed softly. "But you *did* want me."

"You were annoying and I wanted you; Zach was dear; nothing has changed."

Zach

Patrice and Zach made the road trip to Washington in four days and spent the night before the quilt's opening ceremonies in a motel on the edge of the city. The next morning they drove across town to the quilt display, which was being set up on the mall beside the Washington Monument. As they walked up and down walkways exploring the panels, Zach got separated from Patrice and in the jostling crowds had no idea how to begin to find her. He stayed at the panel where he'd last seen her and waited, finally spying her pushing her way frantically through the crowd. "Zach!" She called his name over and over as if there was any chance the boy could hear her. Zach tried to call out and wave to her, but Patrice didn't see him, and the boy's voice was lost over the massive, noisy crowd. Zach made his way slowly to her, stopping just in front of her and touching her arm. "I'm here, Mom."

"Zach!" He was surprised to see that she'd been crying. Her face was rubbery and blotched, and mascara smeared black down one cheek. "I'm so sorry!"

"What?" Lines of people jostled them on the narrow plastic walkway, and Zach tried to take his mom's arm and lead her off of the quilt and out of the crowd.

"I lost you." Patrice started to cry again.

"Yeah."

"I mean I lost *you*."

"I know, Mom."

"I got afraid."

"I know that."

"I'm not talking about this crowd, Zach."

"It's okay." Zach managed to lead Patrice off the quilt and away from all the people. She was shaking. One hand grasped his arm, letting the boy lead her, the other kept reaching across her chest to pat or grasp his shoulder.

"I looked around and you were gone. At first it didn't matter. Then I started to get afraid. Something would happen; someone I didn't know would harm you."

"I'm right here."

"Yes. And the thing already happened—they already happened—those things I wanted to protect you from."

"I'm okay."

Patrice laughed sadly. "You're okay. And you're so big now. Too big now for people to hurt you. Someday no one will hurt you, not even me."

Zach walked her back to the car, unlocked the passenger door, and pushed Patrice gently down and inside. She lay back in the seat, letting her head rest against the top of the seat back, while Zach unlocked the driver's side and slid in behind the wheel. He adjusted the seat backward, making room for his legs, then angled the tilt of the steering wheel upward to give himself more room there as well. Patrice straightened. "What are you doing? You're not old enough to drive."

Zach looked sideways at her. "Josiah taught me years ago. I've been driving since I was eleven."

"Zach . . . I'm so sorry . . . what that man did to you. . . it was my job to protect you . . . but I swear I didn't see it coming."

Zach stared down at his hands gripping the hot steering wheel. He was afraid to look at his mother now.

"I was wrong to run away, Zach."

He inserted the key into the ignition and stopped without cranking it over. "I know you had a hard time, Mom. But you made me pay for it . . . you made me pay." He backed the Valiant out of the parking space and drove slowly down Constitution Avenue. When they had made their way back to Connecticut Avenue and were headed toward the edge of town, Patrice sighed and rubbed her arms fiercely as if trying to wake them up from sleep. "Pull over now. You're not old enough to drive yet."

"I'm good at it."

Patrice laughed. "You are good. And I hope someday you will forgive me."

"Don't."

"I was a bad . . . a lousy mother . . . and so was my mother, and probably her mother too. It's like a sickness in us. People do want to love their children . . ."

Zach pulled off into a Chevron station parking lot. "It's OK. It's OK, Mom. But you're starting to make my stomach hurt now."

The next morning Patrice and Zach returned to the mall just as volunteers were pulling boxes out of trucks and setting folded sections of the quilt in patterns along the plastic walkways. The second day's unfolding ceremony began just after ten. Volunteers dressed entirely in white opened each section together in a formalized ritual that looked like a dance. As each group opened their section of the eighteen-acre quilt, the field before the Washington Monument bloomed like a strange and sorrowful flower. Two hundred thousand visitors walked up and down the rows upon rows, pointing to panels that moved them, or sometimes staring at others in silence.

On a stage in the front, famous politicians, actors, and AIDS activists read a seemingly endless list of the names of the dead. The stage was surrounded by huge loudspeakers, and the names boomed outward, covering the mall with their sound. Someone said there were so many dead it would take two full days to read those pages.

Zach and Patrice found the intake booth for new panels and stood in line with dozens of others, showing off Josiah's panel and talking while the line moved slowly forward and each panel was registered and entered into a special section of the ever-growing quilt.

By two o'clock they lay Josiah's panel in place. Zach brushed the last of the wrinkles from it and backed away slowly, watching strangers begin to walk around it. This was his story—the one he alone could tell. People seemed to smile and point at the colorful Risk map, and Zach wondered if they knew what it all meant—if they could see the thing he knew was true.

Patrice took him to the Smithsonian that afternoon, and they spent hours in the National Museum of Natural History looking at dinosaur skeletons and a huge stuffed blue whale. When they finally left the museum around four, they discovered it had poured rain while they were inside, the quilt had been emergency-folded and stored back in the trucks, the crowds had all gone home, and the only people remaining stood in a small group in the mud before the now-empty stage. Although the electricity had been cut off because of the storm, a dozen people still stood in the rain, reading off the names of the dead which remained.

Zach and Patrice edged closer to the small group in order to hear them, and a woman approached and asked if they would like to read a page. The celebrities had all disappeared with the crowds, and the remaining names were being read by any passing, willing stranger. A young man handed Zach a page. "When you read this," he said kindly, "you can add whatever names you want at the end."

The rain continued in a slow drizzle. Zach walked up to the podium and looked down at the remaining strangers and then beyond them to the devastated field of mud and empty plastic walkways. "Donald Wallace, Scott Finch, Melissa DeSoto, James Lee Dare."

They were simple names, the names of the dead, and yet they held such power. He read the names slowly, and then added Josiah's, and it didn't matter to him that the names were not amplified or heard by two hundred thousand strangers, for when he spoke Josiah's name the wind seemed to lift it, and the words traveled outward like prayers left on mountain prayer flags, forever repeating themselves in the wind.

Zach handed the binder to the next waiting reader and looked for his mother in the small, huddled crowd. He had wanted to add her name to the list, and Dagg's perhaps, and Frank McKinny's. Josiah was dead. A virus had killed him. There were so many kinds of illness; they did so many kinds of harm.

ABOUT THE AUTHOR

Pamela Shepherd's fiction continues to explore the ways in which our histories and our memories shape us. Her work has appeared in *Tasting Life Twice, Passages North,* the *Taos Review, Red Mesa Review,* and *Conceptions Southwest.*

Shepherd graduated from the University of Washington with a BA in philosophy and then completed her MFA in creative writing in 1990. She won the Poets & Writers Writer's Exchange Award for Fiction that year.

In 2001, Shepherd won the Astraea Lesbian Writers Award in Fiction for an excerpt from her novella, *A Little Book of Saints.* She is a student at Pacific School of Religion in Berkeley, California. She is currently completing another novella, entitled *The Formation of Michael Cathcart.*